AF655917

PEARL

SIÂN HUGHES

PICADOR INDIA

First published in 2023 by The Indigo Press,
United Kingdom
First published in India 2023 by Picador India
an imprint of Pan Macmillan Publishing India Private Limited
707 Kailash Building
26 K. G. Marg, New Delhi 110001
www.panmacmillan.co.in

Pan Macmillan, The Smithson, 6 Briset Street, Farringdon,
London EC1M 5NR
Associated companies throughout the world
www.panmacmillan.com

ISBN 978-81-19300-11-2

Copyright © Siân Hughes 2023

This is a work of fiction. Names, characters, businesses, organizations, places, events, and incidents either are the product of the author's imagination or are used fictitiously. Any resemblance to actual persons, living or dead, events, or locales is entirely coincidental.

All rights reserved. No part of this publication may be reproduced, stored in or introduced into a retrieval system, or transmitted, in any form, or by any means (electronic, mechanical, photocopying, recording or otherwise) without the prior written permission of the publisher. Any person who does any unauthorized act in relation to this publication may be liable to criminal prosecution and civil claims for damages.

1 3 5 7 9 8 6 4 2

This book is sold subject to the condition that it shall not, by way of trade or otherwise, be lent, re-sold, hired out, or otherwise circulated without the publisher's prior consent in any form of binding or cover other than that in which it is published and without a similar condition including this condition being imposed on the subsequent purchaser.

Typeset in Goudy Old Style by R. Ajith Kumar, New Delhi
Printed in India by Gopsons Papers Pvt. Ltd., Noida

Praise for *Pearl*

'*Pearl*, an exceptional debut novel, is both a mystery story and a meditation on grief, abandonment and consolation, evoking the profundities of the haunting medieval poem. The degree of difficulty in writing a book of this sort – at once quiet and hugely ambitious – is very high. It's a book that will be passed from hand to hand for a long time to come'

BOOKER PRIZE 2023 JUDGES

'A ghost story, a folk story, a story of loss and familial haunting, Sian Hughes' *Pearl* is an enchanting and eerie exploration of how a child lays down the bones of an ancient past – a medieval poem – as a means of recuperating the voice of lost loved ones. A story about how we tell stories in the face of yawning gaps and deep sorrow'

SALLY BAYLEY

'This is an extraordinary achievement – as a novel, as a meditation on grief and madness, and as a deeply felt, gorgeously imaginative reworking of the 14th-century poem that was its inspiration. Deeply rooted in the flora, fauna, and rituals of the Cheshire village where the author grew up and now lives, it conjures up a world in which paganism and medieval Christianity continue, in their veiled and enigmatic ways, to imbue the contemporary with meaning … It can be read as an utterly gripping psychological mystery … This is, in essence, an elegy of great power, transmogrified into prose'

MAUREEN FREELY

'Haunting, compelling, beautifully written; translates mythic and literary undercurrents into a modern setting'

BERNARD O'DONOGHUE

'Siân Hughes's voice moves us because she manages the difficult art of putting wit to the service of strong feeling – a rare achievement.'

HUGO WILLIAMS

'It's a beautiful, searching novel from start to finish – vividly told and movingly elegiac in its unfolding understanding of the psychology of loss. A terrific achievement'

JANE DRAYCOTT

'Hughes' writing is beautiful, full of details of space and place that give you the sense of being right by Marianne as she lives and breathes. The novel is written in the kind of first person narration that holds your gaze close to whatever the character experiences rather than tells us the story of their lives, with all its accompanying misdirection and philosophising'

RYM KECHACHA

'The prose has a bubbling verve that is deeply appealing'

FINANCIAL TIMES

'Wonderful ... radical in largely dispensing with dramatic tension in order to create a circling story that maps the lasting impact of a loss. The way trauma cuts one off from the world and isolates the sufferer in the moment that hurt them is brilliantly rendered here'

GUARDIAN

'Seamus Heaney Award winner Hughes takes the classic text of the medieval poem *Pearl* as the root for this stunning debut'

SUNDAY POST

'*Pearl* is a novel that has wisdom and experience distilled into it, that defies its downbeat subject matter with the joy of its telling'

TIMES

'Compulsive and wonderfully written, *Pearl* is a small gem'

TIMES LITERARY SUPPLEMENT

Contents

1

The Wakes

Adam and Eve and Pinch-Me
Went down to the river to bathe.
Adam and Eve were drowned
Who do you think was saved?

At the end of every summer I take Susannah back to my home village for a sort of carnival called the Wakes. There's a fancy dress parade and a few fairground rides. A whole ox is roasted on a spit in the playing field. When I was a child there was a thing called the Pram Race. The rules of the race were: a team of two men to push a pram to the next village and back, one running, one in the pram. They both had to drink a pint of beer at every pub along the way. Each two-man team dressed as mother and baby, one of them in a grotesque old nightie filled with balloon breasts, with smeared-on lipstick and hair in curlers, the other in a bib, bonnet and bath-towel nappy.

When they set off, the giant baby would be in the pram pushed by the man in curlers and lipstick, but to stand any chance of winning they needed to take it in turns, so by the first corner they would swap over, the baby leaping out of the pram, the mother leaping in, balloons popping, nappies unravelling, and the bearded baby would take his turn pushing the bearded mother.

There's no pram race now. The roads are too dangerous, so the police stopped it.

The Wakes has been going on here for a long time. It started off as rush-bearing, and that still happens. Back when the churches had floors made of rushes, this was the time of year when they took the old floors out and brought in fresh ones. What we do now is, we dress our family graves in rushes. Halfway down Duckington Lane we pull into a gateway behind the old clay-pigeon shoot, to find some rushes in one of the pits.

We have to change into wellies. I pick up the secateurs from the boot and let the dog out of his travel crate. He straightaway picks up the scent of something and runs in frantic circles just inside the gate. Susannah says thanks, but she'll wait in the car. Cutting rushes isn't fun for her now she's thirteen. I open the back door and ask her again. She sighs, says she might as well, now we're here, puts her phone down and changes into her boots.

Someone's already found all the good ones along the edge. There are hardly any left with nice black tops. Susannah is so light she can step easily over the marshy ground and pick the last few from near the middle. Back in the car I give her the job of plaiting them together with the ribbons. Blue and purple this year. We've brought lavender and mint from the front garden at home to weave in among them. As she twists them together the smell rubs off onto her hands and into the car.

We only need a small bundle. The grave we're dressing is very small. It's not even a grave, strictly. It's a marker stone, and it's not in the place where they buried the ashes. Susannah's made a really nice job of our rushes. Her grandmother would be proud. She's inherited her strong, tiny hands and feet, the red lights in her hair, her sweetly scratchy singing voice.

We get to the church in time for the Wakes service. It's a sort of communal funeral that marks the start of the festival. Everyone who was buried in the parish in that year has their name read out. It's just a list of names. It's beautiful, really, like a poem, an incantation. All those old names from the stones outside, the same families who have lived there forever: Hewitt, Huxley, Leche, Proudlove, another one of their own, late of this parish. Every year I go and listen to it, even though the names that belong to my family have never been read out on that list.

After the service we take our little bundle of rushes round to the back of the church where the graveyard is full of families scrubbing down stones and filling vases and setting out picnic blankets. The thing about the Wakes is, everyone turns up. Some travel a long way. I haven't lived here since I was Susannah's age, and I always come.

I set out our picnic blanket next to the marker stone, unpack the sandwiches and boiled eggs and a twist of salt and pepper. I've made my mother's black-treacle flapjack. I always do. I'm scanning the faces of the people around us, trying to work out who's who by reading the names on the stones next to them, looking into the faces of their children for resemblances from primary school.

I don't believe in the resurrection of the flesh. Not really. But if the dead did peel back the turf and climb out, shaking the earth from their hair, blinking at the sunlight, the scene would not be very different from Wakes weekend in Tilston churchyard. Just a bit more crowded. At the end of every August we're revenants on assorted blankets, sitting on our family graves, the resurrected flesh and bones of our ancestors, wearing their handed-down bad teeth and weak ankles, passing round the sandwiches and cake.

I wonder if the risen dead are supposed to come back the same age as when they died. Good luck for my mother, if they do. Less so for my arthritic great-uncle.

I think of Great-Uncle Matthew, whose marker stone is nearly obliterated in lichen now, next along from the one we're dressing, going up for his afternoon nap in the nursing home, gnarled hand tight on the banister, one step at a time. He'd have trouble getting out of a grave with his poor swollen knees. He always paused partway up the stairs to say, '*Caesar se recipit in hiberna*,' ('Caesar retired to his winter quarters') which he claimed was all he remembered from five years of grammar school. I thought it meant 'I am going to have a nap' until I looked it up in the college library.

None of the others wants to come. My father, my brother. They never do. When I say to them, 'Everyone goes back for the Wakes,' my father gives me his long, sad look. He has been telling me since I was eight years old that my mother is never coming back. He doesn't have to bother with the words now: I know what that look means. But if she did, where else would she try to find us? And how else would she know me except by my sitting on the marker stone, looking more or less as she did thirty years ago? How else would I know her?

If she turned up in the graveyard and needed proof of who I am, I'd sing her a song. I'd sing her 'Green Gravel'. Sometimes I sing it for her, anyway, if I am hanging out washing, or driving alone at night. I think of it as my song, though I am old enough to know now that it is far older than I am, far older than the baby my mother sang it for all those years ago.

Green gravel, green gravel,
Your grass is so green,
The fairest young maiden
That ever was seen.

I'll wash you in new milk
And wrap you in silk,
And write down your name
In a gold pen and ink.

As a child, I had no idea it was a grave she was singing about, a green grave. I thought it was about gravel, the stuff on the drive that washed down the lane when there was a rainstorm. And who is being buried? New milk must be for a newborn infant, the fairest, purest creature, untouched by so much as a minute of life. All the time I thought she was singing it to me, she was singing to that other child, the one with the marker stone the size of a shoebox, a single date on it, birth and death in one.

I find myself starting conversations with her in my head, even now. When I had Susannah, I looked over my shoulder for her, I looked up from my daughter's new face and realised I was looking for my mother's eyes to meet mine, to agree with me she was the fairest young maiden that ever was seen. I waited for her to join in the singing. I started looking around for her, and crying. The midwife asked if there was family history of post-partum psychosis. I said, no. Only grief. There's a family history of grief. You can pass it on. Like immunity, in the milk. Like a song.

2

Charlotte's Web

Cinderella, dressed in yella,
Went to a ball to kiss a fella,
By mistake, kissed a snake,
How many doctors did it take?

I don't remember what happened after I said that. I said a lot of things like it at the time. I was too confused to remember the order of events. Different people came to talk to me. Most of them were kind. Some had the same look I remembered from schoolteachers, police officers, searching my face for the fault line, the wrongness.

(When I was eight I thought they were looking into my face to find the reason my mother disappeared. The terrible thing wrong with me that caused my mother to walk out of the door and never come back. When I grew older I thought they were looking for a resemblance, a danger-sign that I was about to do the same.)

After a few visits their faces all blended into one. I was not really listening to what they had to say. Susannah grew chubby and cheerful, and her cheerfulness rubbed off on me, eventually. It was my job to teach her to smile. I had no choice but to smile myself.

The questions started again last year when Susannah was home from school recovering from tonsillitis. I heard her walking about in the night and went to fetch her a glass of water. I found her sitting in the middle of her bedroom floor cutting her pillow into tiny pieces and arranging them in a circle around her. There was a cloud of tiny feathers drifting around her shoulders like a halo.

'What's the matter?' I said, trying to sound normal. She kept cutting.

'The one with curly hair has been here for hours, and you keep switching the radio on too loud and there's something weird coming out of your feet.'

I felt her head. She'd had a high fever with an ear infection once when she was four, and started jumping on the bed trying to catch the birds in the room, but this time she wasn't even warm. A bit chilly, even, from sitting on the floor in the middle of the night.

The floor shifted under me, and I recognised the feeling, remembered something about my mother, about being in the kitchen with my mother, something about the way she talked sometimes. It was a momentary thing. I could not remember what memory of my mother was summoned by my daughter hallucinating, but the physical sensation was like a drawer sliding open under my feet, then sliding back quickly to catch me in nearly the same spot. Nearly, but not quite, the right spot.

I held my hand against the door frame and concentrated very hard on that piece of painted wood, on my grown-up hand with oil paint under the fingernails, on the colour of the wall behind it chosen by Susannah, the name of the colour on the tin, ocean breeze. I handed her the glass of water, and went downstairs to call the out-of-hours GP.

This time I was ready for their questions. I was able to look them in the eye and say, 'My mother walked out when I was eight years old, and she has never been found. My brother was a baby. No, she had never been diagnosed with anything, because she hid from doctors. She hid from everyone. She home-schooled me because, well, I don't know. So, yes, there is a family history. Of madness.' This time I gave it a different name. Madness? Grief? I was talking about the same thing.

I felt treacherous, mentioning the home-schooling. I found myself answering the next question before anyone said it out loud. Why? Why did she keep me at home? People always asked what was the matter with her. What was she afraid of? I don't know. Big buildings? Teachers? Other parents? Leaving the house? No one ever asked the questions I want to answer: What did you do all day? What did she teach you? What was it like?

She read me the Fall of Jericho in the King James Bible, *Alice in Wonderland*, *The Little Princess*, we grew runner beans up the staircase, made insect houses out of balsa wood, we sang all the verses to 'The Raggle Taggle Gypsies', sewed dolls out of cloth and baptised them in the stream, we kept rabbits and ducklings and picked buckets of raspberries and made stained-glass windows out of pastry and boiled sweets.

My first experiences of school confirmed my suspicion that

life was better at home, and if anyone asks me now, why were you home-schooled, I have taught myself to say, because my mother was really good at it. And, as it turned out, I didn't have much time with her, so I am glad, now, that we spent all those days together. It took me until I was well into my thirties, and a mother myself, to learn to think this way, to be brave enough to stand up for her, to stand up for my right to a positive memory of my mother.

When someone takes their life, they don't only steal the future out from under our feet, they also desecrate their past. It makes it hard to hold on to the good things about them. And no one deserves to be judged on the worst five minutes of their life, even if those five minutes turn out to be their last.

I wanted to talk to her so many times when Susannah was little. To tell her when Susannah learned a new word, or did up a button for the first time, or put her shoes on by herself. To ask her stupid things like, do you think I could put spinach into this rice porridge? Would it taste disgusting?

I still want to turn to her now. I'd like to tell her, there's another name for it, there's no need to live your whole life feeling that frightened. You can take pills for it, and make a wellness recovery plan, and meet with your key worker and tell your consultant if you are still seeing angels on the stairs.

I'd like to tell her, being ill is not your fault. I remember you as you were. At your very best. I remember your garden, the long kitchen table where we made potato prints and gingerbread shapes and the window seat where you read me *Charlotte's Web* to distract me from picking at my chickenpox.

I remember the words to 'Green Gravel'. I remember salt patterns on the floor to keep the devil at bay, bottles of seaweed hanging in the kitchen window to ward off evil spirits, sucking the taste of salt dough off my fingers, the smell of coal tar soap in the downstairs bathroom, the scrape of the back door on the ridge in the stone floor. I keep it all safe in me. I swallow every inch of it. I refuse to let any of it go.

The house was full of secrets: generations of additions and revisions, steps up and down between rooms, stubbornly cold corners, at least four different shapes of window. Great-Uncle Matthew gave it to my parents as a wedding present, the crumbling house, and a barn full of his abandoned inventions, many of them adaptations of gardening and other tools for wheelchairusers and amputees.

My mother turned her back on the house and cut six-footsquare herb beds in a perfect grid from a corner of the walled orchard. She had lived above a shop all her life: she had no idea how things grew. She planted randomly, at any time of year, and the squares of herbs mixed themselves with each other or went to seed or rotted, as the fancy took them.

Long before we left it, my mother's garden had gone wild. It does not take long for the ground to reclaim its own. If a weed is simply a plant in the wrong place, then everything in my mother's garden became a weed in the years we waited in that house for her to return. Or perhaps there's no simple before and after picture. Perhaps the plants were always doing as they liked, even under her care.

We did not mean to let it all go to ruin, piles of rotting grasses blocking the paths, the edges of the beds all softened and smudged. But we did not try very hard to stop it either. We let the apples fall from the trees and collect wasps in the grass while we ate sweet things out of plastic pots that she would have hated.

We gave up her ban on television, and on junk food. It felt like a dare. Something like a bad spell to bring her back, furious, to put everything right. It felt like my own anger, too, to wear nightdresses with Disney characters on them, and play with plastic ponies with rainbow tails, to eat fish and chips in the car sitting in the drive because we couldn't be bothered to carry them across the yard in the rain.

We failed to tell Joe about her. We sang him the songs to adverts and left *The Lion King* on repeat. We failed to bring him up the way she would have wanted. When we taught him to speak we left her out of his vocabulary. He was our safe place, our blank slate, our elf of forgetfulness, and we held him up as protection against the world. Now I feel guilty that I did not try to keep her in his mind.

When we did start to talk about her again, we had left too long a gap. Our stories no longer matched perfectly, and no one was sure which was the right version. I am not sure, now, what I am remembering of her, and what I am remembering of someone else's story.

I didn't have chickenpox until I started school, which would make sense. Where else would I have caught it? But who was reading *Charlotte's Web* to me on the window seat, keeping my poor scabby hands away from my face? Did my father take time off work? Or was it one of our childminders? Was I even on the window seat? I remember it having blue willow-pattern cushions. My father says he doesn't remember having any blue willow pattern in the old house. He thinks the window seats were velvet.

Even the 'Raggle Taggle Gypsies' song is open to debate. I know I acted it out, running away across the garden, riding my tree-trunk horse, lying in the long grass to sing, 'Tonight I'll lie in a wide open field, along with the raggle taggle gypsies-oh!'

I remember 'Oh what care I for my high-heeled shoes, a-made of Spanish leather-oh!' I remember taking a pair of shoes from my mother's wardrobe and flinging them into the potato patch, then having to go out and track them down by torchlight. But my father says she never had any high-heeled shoes. And why would she send me out to get them after dark? Where would she be going? It makes no sense.

I know it makes no sense. A new mother walking out of the kitchen door leaving her baby asleep in his Moses basket and never coming back. Not even stopping to close the door behind her.

I claim all that I can rescue of the time before. Even if someone else tells me the details are wrong, or in the wrong order. Because it is mine. Blue willow pattern in the window seat. *Charlotte's Web*. Gingerbread people with currant buttons. Runner beans up the stairways. High heels kicked off in the potato patch, riding my tree-trunk horse.

My mother's minty, leafy smell on her hands as she tucked me into bed, teasing me by singing, 'Oh what care I for my goose-feather bed, with the sheets turned down so bravely-oh!' All my life I've turned down my sheets so bravely-oh. I have shaken out many a brave sheet, tucked in many a brave corner, over the years, and her voice has sung me through it. I have often needed to be brave.

3

Nine Beads at a Time

One, two, three, four, five, six, seven,
All good children go to heaven.
Penny on the water,
Tuppence on the sea,
Thruppence on the railway,
Out goes SHE!

The one place where I can picture my mother clearly, and be absolutely sure it is an image from my own mind, is in the orchard. She is sitting under one of the apple trees for shade, which is very sharp around her, so I know it is summer. One of the kitchen chairs is tucked under a tree, and next to it is her red-and-gold raffia sewing basket. She is sewing name tapes onto grey school uniforms.

I am spying on her from inside a herb bed. The plant is a kind of spurge. The seed pods warm up and tighten and thin in the sun until they pop, sending the seeds out in a shower.

I am racing two of them, betting on the one next to me to be the first to pop.

There is a rug on the ground near to her, with some plates on it. I have taken a spoon with jam on it and I am licking it clean where I am sitting. My mother says, 'Marianne, don't put that back into the jar now you've licked it.' I believed my mother had supernatural powers of sight and hearing. She encouraged this belief. Especially when it came to my helping myself to food.

There is a pile of grey tunics and red cardigans and round-collared school blouses on the ground where she has finished sewing in my name. If I am good she will let me play with the leftover name tapes: with their curly red script they make excellent doll's bandages in toy hospitals. Tiny dots of felt pens fill up the gaps and look wonderfully gory.

This could be any summer from when I was four to when I was eight. I am guessing this is when I am seven, the year I read *Harriet the Spy* – I spent a lot of that summer spying on my parents from the spurge beds. Every year the uniforms would appear in a huge green plastic bag, every year she would sit in the garden and sew them with my name, then they would be hung in the landing cupboard ready for September. Sometimes I was allowed to dress up in the complete outfit and parade in front of my father. But I never went to school.

Every year my father's birthday would come round in the middle of September, and somehow I would still be at home. I did ask one year if I could go. So I was taken to play with a family nearby, who had a daughter called Pippa at the village school. She had a special room called a playroom and six very thin dolls with long, matted hair and lots of different outfits.

I was especially impressed with their shoes. None of my dolls had shoes. I asked Pippa what her parents were called. She said, 'Who?'

'Your parents, your mum and dad. What are their names?'

She looked blank. Then she said, 'They don't have names. Only Mummy and Daddy.' I laughed out loud.

'But what about when they were children? They must have had names, when they were babies, even!' She looked blank again.

When my mother came to take me home Pippa was still angry with me. In the car on the way home my father asked if I would like to go to school with Pippa. I said, 'I don't think she's very good at conversation, but her dolls are very nice.' My parents exchanged a long look. I knew it meant I was not going to school. Something to do with the word 'conversation'. I checked the next day and the uniform cupboard was empty again.

I have no idea what happened to all those school clothes. They couldn't have returned them to the shop, with my name sewn inside them all. When I finally did go to school, at the wrong time of year, carelessly, because no one could work out what else to do with me, we could not find so much as a white sock or a red cardigan anywhere. The landing cupboard was full of sheets and towels and outgrown baby clothes. My father seemed as puzzled as anyone. How had she hidden them? She couldn't drive. How would she donate them? Did she burn them? I had to go in the middle of the week, in the middle of a term, in my bright green corduroy jeans with the pink heart-shaped patches on the knees and my home-knitted jumper with rows of colourful beads in loops around the cuffs. By the time we had sat in the head teacher's office with my father trying to fill in the forms while Joe cried and spat out his dummy, it was halfway through maths. I followed the head teacher into the classroom and stood in front of the teacher's desk. Everyone stopped talking.

The other children stared at me. I knew why they were staring. They were wondering what was wrong with me. I was wondering myself. I could tell by their faces that they thought it was because of my funny clothes and my hair falling out of its bad plaits that my father did not know how to do up tightly, and the teacher could tell that too. When she said, 'I am sure we would all love to have a special jumper like that, Marie,' I knew for a fact I was bad. I was so bad I had to have my name cut short, and my jumper wrongly made. I didn't even correct her on my name.

She said, as I had missed so much, starting school now, perhaps it would be better for me to sit with the younger children. I towered over the other children at my table, an awkward giant in my colourful clothes, and found that none of them were any good at conversation. I realised right away that invisibility was the only way to survive there, and being taller by a head and shoulders than all the others at your table, with a name that is too long for the teacher to bother with, and beads on your cuffs that click and jingle against the table top, makes you bad, bad, bad.

I wouldn't have stayed long on the tiny infant table, bashing my knees against the underside of my desk, if only I hadn't forgotten how to read. I remembered the things I had read before she left. I knew by heart the Ladybird history book about Elizabeth Fry and the prisons. I could describe the urchin Smith and all his layers of clothes printed onto his skin because he had never taken any of them off. But I couldn't work out why none of the words on the pages they gave me at school made any sense to me. Was it some kind of trick?

I said I only knew how to read English, like in the books at home. Could I bring those instead? And even when it was proved to me they hadn't been playing some kind of cruel game, that it was my own mind that had done this to me, I never lost my suspicion of them. I still looked at them sideways from under my too-long fringe and muttered spells to protect me from their disapproval.

For the first time, too, I knew that no one in my family would understand a word of what I needed to say about it. Once I arrived at school, I was on my own. I learned to shrug, and say it was alright, really, I supposed, that I could not remember what I had eaten, or read, or what we were learning. It was all beyond them.

I had to learn to put my hand up to ask things. To practise, I put my hand up a lot, but then had nothing to say, or nothing in particular. So I asked to go to the toilet. The toilets were in a block behind the main building, up two concrete steps. The cubicles had huge green wooden doors, and heavy bolts that caught my fingers. I sat there letting my bottom go numb with cold, waiting until the teacher sent 'someone sensible' to bring me back.

I chewed the loops of beads on my cuffs, sitting there, and when the thread snapped between my teeth, I swallowed the beads in sets of nine, counting them with my tongue against the roof of my mouth. Sometimes I sat there long enough that some of the beads from the day before would come out the other end, embedded in shit, and I watched them disappear down the pipe.

When I broke the first set, I worried what my mother would say when she came home and found I had broken my jumper. All last winter she had knitted it for me, so I would not be jealous of all the things she was making for the new baby. We had sat together in our favourite corner of the sofa and I helped arrange the beads in sequences of nines from the sorting tray we had made out of an old Rice Krispies box. Then I thought, when she saw the jumper she would understand how upset I was at school, and I wouldn't have to go there any more. I would get out the Rice Krispies box sorting tray, and we'd sit together stitching it all back perfectly until there was no trace left of the time we had been apart.

But then the next little loop of nine beads went down the drain, and the next, and still she had not come home to mend it. Once the cuffs came undone, the edges of the sleeves started to unravel in long lines up to the elbow. Now I knew I was a bad daughter. I had broken the special jumper she had made for me, and there would never be another one. Because she was never coming home.

4

Boiling the Kettle Dry

Oh dear me
Mother caught a flea
Put it in the teapot
To make a cup of tea.
The flea jumped out
And made her shout
In came Daddy
With his shirt hanging out.

I can pinpoint the exact moment the police stopped looking for a missing woman and started looking for a dead body. One that, by now, was probably beyond recognition. It was the day they stopped phoning my father to tell him they had found 'someone' and started to say 'something'. Something in woodland. Something in the river. Something.

He would go off with them then, to see what they had found. Lindsey would come and babysit, or her sister Mel, or both of them, if it was night time, because they found the place spooky, they said. They brought cakes from the shop, or colourful biscuits, made me hot chocolate and let me stay up late watching programmes with detectives in them. I thought for years they did that on purpose. Edward would go off with the police and I would watch some show where the detective always solves the case. It didn't occur to me until much later it was simply what they watched on the television in the evening. The kind of thing that was on after I was usually in bed.

When Edward got home he would shake his head, and no one would say anything at all. Now he says he has regrets about all those times he went, and met other families, other husbands or wives or parents or grown-up children, all going to see if this was the something they were waiting for. He regrets letting them all go without talking to them, asking for their addresses, promising to keep in touch, keep asking, did you find her yet? Find him yet? Form a support group. Go on annual picnics. But he didn't. Something stopped him looking them in the eye and asking, who are you here for? Something stopped them looking him in the eye and asking him the same.

When he came back I wanted him to bring me back their stories. The stories of why they were there, who they were looking for, who was missing from their lives. I wanted to know, how did they lose them? Did they go out shopping together and lose them in the car park? Did they go on holiday and lose them at the beach? Did they lose them at home, like us? Were they wearing their coats, or just jumpers? Did they take a bag of things? Did they have any money with them? Did they have anywhere else to go?

I collected stories of loss, abandonment, shame. Susannah's

father was the first one to give me a proper disappearance story. The way I remember it, I was in love with him long before he told me about his mother's disappearance. Perhaps he had some signal my radar picks up, some badge of abandonment. His mother left, and when he asked when she would be coming back, his father opened the huge wardrobes in their bedroom. They were empty. 'That was where she kept her clothes,' he said. 'So I assume she's not coming back.' The big reveal. The few remaining coat hangers gently clicking together as the door opens wide. The smell of wood, and nothing else. He was exactly the same age as I was when my mother left. He had a perfect memory of her disappearance. Not the moment she set off, perhaps, but certainly the moment he knew. I had nothing. I have, I admit, been tempted to borrow his version. It is so much better than mine.

What do I remember? I remember the police coming to the house. The older one was with Edward, and the younger one sat at the kitchen table and looked at his hands. He had a row of spots on his neck where his collar had rubbed the skin. I was standing behind his chair next to the stove, and wondering how to put the kettle on. I had never put the kettle on before. I was not allowed to touch the stove. But I knew that was what you were supposed to do when someone came to the house and sat at the kitchen table as if they were waiting for something.

Joe was crying in his Moses basket on the kitchen floor. I was not allowed to pick him up on my own. This was a much stricter rule than the one about the kettle. No one had specifically forbidden me to put the kettle on. There had never been any need. But the rule about the baby was very clear. I was allowed to stroke his face and try to distract him with a toy or a rattle. I was allowed to sing him a song and hold his hand. But not to pick him up.

The kitchen floor was huge uneven stone slabs. If my mother happened to be in the bathroom or upstairs somewhere or hanging washing out in the garden or answering the telephone in the hall when Joe started to cry, then I was on no account to pick him up. He is safe in his basket. Crying will not hurt him like the floor could hurt him. Kiss him on the feet so you don't give him a cold. The changing mat goes on the floor, never on a table. Don't put anything in his mouth in case he swallows it. Wash your hands with soap.

So I sat down next to the basket while he cried and tried to sing to him and kiss his feet through his Babygro and play peekaboo. He cried louder and louder, and the kettle boiled and boiled and the steam filled the room. It was the kind of kettle that sits on top of the stove, and it didn't switch itself off. I have no idea how long that went on. Not long, I suppose. I don't remember if Edward came back in and lifted off the kettle, or if the policeman eventually got up and did it himself.

I don't know which of them picked up the baby. I have an image of Edward walking up and down the kitchen with the baby on his shoulder, Joe's square body the size of Edward's hand as he patted him, the hiccupping and gulping as the milk came back up and trickled down the back of Edward's jacket. But which day does that image belong to? How many times did I see the same thing? Every day. For a long time. I have no idea which day's memory belongs in what order.

Why didn't I notice she had gone? The very minute, the second she was out of the door? It troubled me for years. What if I had seen her, and followed her? What if I had asked her to come back inside and see my cutting-out? Or asked her to help me make a pipe-cleaner doll? What if I had caught up with her as she walked down the footpath to the river? She left her wellies behind. What if I had run after her in my good shoes, and got them covered in mud? Would she have turned us both round and taken me back to get changed? Possibly.

She didn't leave us on our own. I don't want you thinking that. Mrs Wynne was there. All that year Mrs Wynne was there, to help because of the new baby. She arrived after lunch. Then my mother took Joe up to her room for a feed and a nap, and I did something quietly so as not to disturb them. Mrs Wynne folded up piles of baby clothes and put away dishes and kept me company while I copied out poetry in my handwriting book. Sometimes she played snakes and ladders with me.

She did not run the hoover in case it woke them upstairs. She mopped the floor and peeled potatoes for supper. When she leaned over she had brown stocking tops under her skirt. She tied a tea towel round my middle for an apron, and let me help her make fairy cakes. Her arms were soft and cakey when she tucked the tea towel into my jeans, and she smelled of vanilla. Nothing seemed to surprise her. A double six in snakes and ladders. A double-yolker egg in the mix.

When my mother and Joe came downstairs Mrs Wynne would make a pot of tea, sit and drink a cup with my mother while they admired the baby and I showed my mother what I had been doing, and then Mrs Wynne would cycle her slow wobbly cycling back up the lane. In bad weather she wore a plastic rain hat over her perm. I don't know how long she usually stayed. An hour or two.

I cannot tell you when my mother left, not exactly. Sometime in the afternoon. By the time I realised something had gone seriously wrong, Mrs Wynne had called Edward home from work early, because it was time for her to go home herself and she didn't know where my mother had gone. I don't remember going from room to room looking for her. I don't remember Mrs Wynne going upstairs to fetch the Moses basket down from the bedroom when Joe woke up. I don't remember running round the garden calling her name in the rain. I don't remember any of that, but I suppose it must have happened.

I remember Mrs Wynne on the phone to Edward, how she had to ask the office for Dr Brown. She said something like, 'I'm sorry, perhaps she told me about an appointment or something. But I can't remember her saying anything.' I remember the air in the room around us changing texture as Mrs Wynne was talking, setting like jelly so that everything wobbled if you looked at it too long. The words were no longer normal words. The air around the telephone had gone slippery with them.

I remember waiting by the front window, watching for Edward's car. I remember Mrs Wynne's face turning away from me already, the shame of it filling the air. Even before Edward arrived we had lost the ability to look into each other's eyes. We were both there. We lost her. The shame filled up the house room by empty room, a huge squashy balloon of it, sucking the air out of everywhere so we couldn't breathe.

When Edward got back Mrs Wynne offered to stay and help while he waited for her to come home, but he called for a taxi so she wouldn't have to cycle in the dark. He said, 'I'm sure it's some kind of misunderstanding.' But Mrs Wynne was looking down at the floor, as if what we had was catching. As if a single beam of light from one set of eyes to another might carry the shame of our badness, our bad luck. Night fell, and there was still no word from her, so he called the police.

Joe couldn't have been crying in his basket on the kitchen floor all evening. He would only have been there for a few minutes while Edward stepped outside to talk to the police officer where his daughter could not hear what they were saying. But what I remember is the baby crying, the parents gone, the man in uniform sitting in his cloud of steam not knowing what to do. That becomes the dramatic image, the empty wardrobe, the moment of departure.

Edward tried his hardest to talk to the police outside the door, or in another room, but it was evening now, and Joe kept crying. He always cried in the evenings. My mother used to call it six o'clock colic, and if I pointed out it was nearly quarter to eight, for instance, she would say, 'Well, he's too young to tell the time.' I kept going to fetch Edward, to get him to walk Joe up and down, which usually helped. So despite all his efforts to keep me from the conversation, I heard the most important part.

The policeman asked if Edward thought his wife was in a state of mind where she was a danger to herself. Edward said no, definitely not. He would not have gone to work if he thought for a moment she, no, not at all.

And the policeman said very quietly, 'You see, Mr Brown, if we are told she is in danger, if she is in a dangerous state of mind, we can start to look for her.'

There was a long pause. Edward was not looking at the policeman. He was walking up and down by the kitchen window, jiggling Joe on his shoulder. He kept rocking to and fro, patting Joe's back. When he turned around, his face was very white and sharp under his eyes, the skin pulled tight.

'I see,' he said. 'Very well. I believe my wife was in a dangerous state of mind this afternoon when she left the house.' The policeman turned his little black shiny notebook over and snapped the elastic band tight around it.

I remember what we ate for tea that night. Fish fingers and beans. I remember the rain. The police who came to the house were all soaked from walking up the lane, their feet covered in mud. Except we never ate fish fingers and beans until Lindsey came to look after us. And the rain had stopped. When they asked if her coat was missing, I remember saying, but it stopped raining today, a bit, I think. She might not need it. At least let's allow me the rain. I dismiss the fish fingers. I don't have much left. Let's allow me the rain.

5

The Laws of Physics

Mother's in the kitchen
Doin' a bit of stitchin'
In comes a bogeyman
To push her OUT!

If you head out of our village down the lower road to the old watermill, you come alongside a row of dark ugly ponds we called the pits. They are surrounded by trees, some half-fallen in, and the surface is greasy with dead leaves. When I first learned to ride a bike we would come along here, my mother in front, going very slowly to allow me to keep up. She had to keep looping back or wobbling into the middle of the lane to wait for me. When we came to the pits she would cycle on the wrong side of the road, far away from them. It didn't matter. There were hardly ever any cars.

Every time we went past she would tell me the place was haunted, which was why she kept as far away from the water as she could. She told me how, years ago, a beautiful girl was walking home along this lane after the Wakes, and a young boy followed her, perhaps, some say he did, some say he didn't, and she was found drowned in the pit. The reason it was haunted was he was never punished. No one was punished. So she can never be at rest.

And then further on down the lane my mother would loop back around on her bike and cycle alongside me and say, perhaps they were punished, in the end, because that man grew old in a cottage not far from our house, and by the time he died the whole place was grown over with hawthorn like Sleeping Beauty's castle. Those creepers worked their way into the windows and doors, wrapping themselves around the porch so it fell away from the front of the house, the garden a mass of thorns you had to cut your way out of. Nothing would stop those thorns from growing stronger and stronger the more you cut them.

When the old man lay dying he called for his brother, claiming that he had something important to say, and the brother had to take a ladder and lean it up to the bedroom window to hear him because his wife never would let him in the door, but it was too late. And all the years he lived in that house with his wife there was never a child. Not one.

I knew she meant the thorns were the dead girl come back to find him, they were her fingers climbing into him, breaking down the mortar and sucking the life out of the house, that it was the dead girl who stopped the babies from coming to that house. I asked her, had she seen the house with the creepers, was it still there? She said, yes, we go past it all the time but you would hardly notice it now it is so fallen in and grown over.

The garden is full of rhubarb and raspberries gone to seed, and some people go in through where the hedge is collapsed and help themselves. I would never go in it myself, she would say. I would never SET FOOT.

I was terrified of the pits. Each time we cycled past I would imagine the girl floating in the water, her long dress ballooning out, her poor cold feet sticking up out of the water all yellow, her face hidden in the peaty scum. I could barely keep my eyes looking straight ahead, and drifted out into the middle nearer to where my mother cycled along the opposite ditch. Sometimes she would let me hold on to the rack on the back of her bike and be pulled along and out under the trees that closed over the lane, away from the darkness and coldness that belonged in that place.

When did they first tell me they thought she had drowned? Not right away. Weeks certainly, maybe months after she stepped outside. I didn't believe them. I said, 'No! She always cycles on the other side of the road, she would never SET FOOT. She hated that place, where the girl drowned.' And all the time I was saying, 'No, no, no!' it sounded to me like my voice was going further and further away, smaller and smaller into the distance until I was shouting silently into a long thin tube. All around the tube was darkness, but at the end of the tunnel was a bright, lit circle of water with a girl lying face down in it.

I didn't know that I was passing out. I had heard the word fainting. But no one had ever described what that might feel like if it happened to me. I thought this sudden loss of hearing down to the most distant whisper, this reduction in what I could see to a small far-away circle, were permanent losses. I thought in that moment that I would never again see or hear anything the way I used to. And in a way I was right.

I blacked out onto the stone floor in the kitchen, knocked out the last of my milk teeth, and gave myself mild concussion. I was glad of it. It stopped them talking about the water, for one thing. And I very quickly discovered that this was a way to avoid going to school. Each morning I was asked if I still had a headache. If I had a headache I was allowed to stay in bed and eat Marmite sandwiches and leave the crusts and draw pictures and look out of the window.

After a week or so the doctor came to visit me. He said it was unusual for someone my age to still be suffering from concussion after this long. That maybe I ought to go for an X-ray. That I had no other symptoms, no dizziness or sickness, but that maybe they ought to check. He said all this to my father in the doorway, and so handed me some useful weapons in my fight against school. Dizziness, sickness. When I ran out of headaches I tried these out. I was too cunning to use the doctor's exact words. I experimented with different ways to describe dizziness. 'I feel like I am on a roundabout and I can't get off,' or 'Everything spins around me.'

Mostly Edward shrugged and said, 'Me too, sweetie,' and let me lie in bed. I realised that almost any physical symptom could now be attributed to my mother's disappearance. Headaches, sickness, sleeplessness, sleepiness, dirty fingernails, eczema patches, a snotty nose, tooth decay, unbrushed hair, nits. Especially nits. Nothing was off-limits.

Around the time I passed out on the kitchen floor Lindsey came to look after Joe every day so Edward could go back to work. If I claimed to be ill, all he had to do was tell Lindsey I was staying home, and get out of there.

I adored Lindsey. She painted bright colours on my chewed fingernails. She let me stroke her fluffy yellow jumper. She brushed my hair so much it stood up in static fluff, and tried to plait it flat. She didn't try to tell me freckles were beautiful, or that my hair looked nice. She said, 'You can put on foundation when you're older, if you want. Some highlights might help.'

She kept the electric fire on all day, and the television, and she didn't mind how many times Joe watched the same episode of *Thomas the Tank Engine*. She made us things to eat out of cardboard boxes in the freezer. She read my horoscope in her magazines and it was always about boyfriends. She talked to her sister on the phone for hours with the receiver tucked between her shoulder and her ear while she carried Joe on one hip. She was so skinny his legs wrapped right around her. She smelled of Dolly Mixture and apple peel. Any time she put Joe down he cried, so she carried him around all day. She could put make-up on with one hand while Joe balanced on her waist. She let him hold the little tubes of paint for her. She had a special brush for putting powder on her face and she tickled my nose with it.

If I drew her a picture she said, 'Oh, you are good with your hands. I bet you got that from your mother, bless her.' I don't think my mother ever drew or painted, but I took the compliment anyway. I liked to get her talking about my mother, even though she'd never met her. I would bring her random things from around the house and say it was my mother's favourite, or that she had made it, or found it in the garden. Half the time I made it up.

When the school attendance lady eventually came round I was lying on the sofa in my pyjamas, watching *Pigeon Street* on our new television, eating sliced-bread sandwiches with ready-sliced cheese. The attendance lady was dressed head to foot in shiny brown things. Shiny brown shoes, shiny pale brown tights, a shiny brown polo neck jumper, a shiny brown skirt that creaked. I guess it must have been leather. I had never seen anything like it before. Lindsey tidied up an armchair and offered her tea. Lindsey asked how she liked her tea. I answered for her. 'Brown,' I said. 'She likes her tea brown.' I thought this was quite funny.

The brown lady opened her shiny brown handbag and took out a notebook and pen. 'So,' she said, snapping the bag shut again, 'I understand you recently lost your mother. Is that right?' It was perhaps the first time anyone described it that way. I had carelessly, foolishly, lost my mother. I had failed to keep hold of her and let her slip away. I had been playing a game in the garden with her, and forgotten where I put her. I had stopped thinking about her for a minute, then remembered too late.

I realised now why the police had asked me so many questions. Where had I been, what had I been doing, what time was it when? All the questions you ask someone who has lost something. Where did you last see it? Did you take it outside with you?

It was one of the things that maddened me about my parents. If I said to either one of them, 'I can't find my shoe,' or teddy or cardigan, they would say, 'It's exactly where you left it.' If pushed, Edward liked to say, 'According to the laws of physics, Marianne, matter can be neither created nor destroyed. It has therefore not disappeared from the face of the earth.'

I narrowed my eyes at the brown lady, and concentrated on not crying. I tried hard to rub out the picture in my head of my mother saying, 'Think, Marianne! I must be exactly where you left me. Where did you leave me this time? Where could I be? Have you left me in the garden maybe?' I swallowed hard and said, 'According to the laws of physics, matter can neither be created nor destroyed.' I kept staring at her very hard to prove I was not really crying even though my face was quite wet.

She looked at me a long time before replying. What she said was, 'What are you reading at the moment?' As if everyone over the age of six is reading something at the moment. I was having a lot of trouble reading, so I told her the last thing I remembered reading when my mother was there. The Fall of Jericho. The army marched around and around the walls, with their feet keeping perfect time, until the walls simply crumbled. She asked me if I thought that really happened. And I said, yes, why not? How else do you get the walls around a city to all fall down?

'Oh, I don't know,' she said, 'maybe some kind of explosive?' I quite liked the brown lady after that. Which is a good job, as she came to visit me a lot.

I developed a fine collection of symptoms. I tuned into all medical stories. Lindsey was a wonderful source of unsuitable material. Most of her stories involved mysterious blood loss and drinking things you shouldn't. I even tried, 'I think I drank too much last night. My head is killing me.' I had no idea why my father thought that was funny. Or why he sent me to school the day I said, 'It's my time of the month again.'

And, like a lot of hypochondriacs, I was frequently, coincidentally, ill. I caught up with all the childhood illnesses

I had missed while staying at home. It seemed like every time I was dragged back to the classroom I caught another one. The odd thing is, I don't remember feeling any different staying home all day when I was actually ill. I watched television. I drew pictures. I built countless wooden towers for Joe to knock down, I made circles of wooden train track around the striped rug in the living room, while he crawled behind me taking it apart. Sometimes I had horrible spots, or swollen glands, or a headache, or a snotty nose. Sometimes I didn't. When anyone asked me how I was feeling I answered honestly, 'Horrible.'

I never again tried out the line about matter neither being created nor destroyed. My father had stopped saying it. So I worked out it had been a lie. Like so many certainties of the world before she left, it turned out to be a trick. Matter most definitely could be destroyed. It was entirely possible to lose something. Permanently. Remembering where you last saw it was no help at all. And even the things you held on to, kept in your sight, might change unrecognisably into something else.

Your baby brother might smell of new clothes and special eczema creams, of baby wipes and orange food in a jar. He might grow out of all recognition even as you stayed at home watching his every move. Your kitchen might smell of chewing gum and hairspray and tinned beans. All the plants on the windowsill could turn into dead brown stalks. Your bed might not feel like your bed. You might wake up in it one day and find it has a new cover with a picture of a multicoloured horse on it and the sheets aren't stripy and fluffy any more, they are smooth and shiny and pink. Your house might stop sounding of radio voices and start to sound like the television adverts for teabags or pilchards or breakaway biscuits.

Your garden might be full of people in uniforms, the pathways all trodden out, the weeds taken over, the gravel in the driveway scrunched aside by too many cars and washed down to the bridge at the bottom of the lane. One morning you wake up and find your hair is falling out, and when it comes back it is the wrong colour. Suddenly your father, who was of no particular age yesterday, is an old man. He used to be Daddy, but suddenly there are lots of new people in the house and they all call him Edward, so you start to do the same. You never used to think about him dying, but now it's something you have to consider. Every matter can be destroyed. Everything that matters.

6

Creatures of the Air

As I went over the water,
The water went over me.
I saw two little blackbirds
Sitting in a tree.

One called me a rascal,
One called me a thief,
So I took up my little black stick
And knocked out all their teeth.

Now here is a thing about birds. Great-Uncle Matthew, who gave my parents the house in the village, was really my great-great-uncle, but that is too much of a mouthful. And when Uncle Matthew was very old, Edward would take me to visit him in the nursing home where he got lighter and lighter until he just evaporated. Flew away. His shoulders curved forward and his arms folded like wings on the coverlet, his fingers nothing more than brown feathers curled into the palm.

I was very young when he died, but I remember the visits. We took him flowers from the garden, fairy cakes I had helped to decorate, my paintings, coconut ice. One time we made fudge. I liked him. He could only talk out of one side of his mouth, and he could only use one hand, and he smelled very clean, of pyjamas fresh from the drawer, and his thick, white hair was brushed back from his forehead and reached right down past his ears.

He taught me silly rhymes. I liked best the one about the knights of old best. I thought it was about him.

In days of old when knights were bold
They wore bright shining armour
But now the nights are dark and cold
They wear Marks and Sparks pyjamas.

He was a knight but unfortunately the nursing home had mislaid his bright shining armour, or left it to rust in the garden, and now he had to be my bright shining knight in his ironed pyjamas. He knew another one about knights.

One fine day in the middle of the night
Two dead men got up to fight.
Back-to-back they faced each other,
Drew their swords and shot each other.

So I knew he specialised in knights. I worked out he secretly was one. He was in disguise in his pyjamas because he had to get up in the middle of the night to do his fighting. It made perfect sense to me. He died when I was four.

Edward took him to the hospital to look at the last scans of his bones, and they were full of holes. Great-Uncle Matthew said they looked like bird bones. The cancer had eaten them away until they were full of tiny pockets of air, bubbles in lemonade, a speckled scan of hollow, empty bones ready to fly to their maker.

And when his body was brought to the church the night before the funeral, my mother felt sorry for him, all alone in the cold on his last night above ground, and she went to the church after dark to sit with the coffin. As she walked down the aisle three black birds flew out of the tower, screaming. They dived down onto her head and arms, pecking at her and shrieking into her face. Edward said she ran all the way home, and the cuts on her face and forearms were real enough.

The next day they went back for the funeral but the birds were nowhere to be seen. And when Edward picked up the coffin to carry it out to the graveyard he said it felt as if there was nothing inside it. It was a wicker coffin like one of those big picnic baskets, or a pigeon carrier. The weight of a soul, however many grams it is, was gone. He said when he helped lower it down into the ground he felt maybe he ought to check that there really was something inside it. But he didn't.

My mother believed in angels. She saw them all the time. She said they especially loved the stairs under the long window. She put little models of them all over the house. Over each doorway. On the landing there was a whole collection of them. She liked wooden carved ones, plaster ones, even plastic models from cheap nativity cribs. She liked the chubby baby ones and the long, curved ones like slim girls with their folded wings and downward-cast eyes.

After the fire, I wanted to know if the angels had been rescued. Edward had saved a box of them, the wooden ones mostly. The plaster ones had got so dirty with smoke it would ruin them to scrub them clean, and most of the pictures were damp or speckled or just not worth bothering with. I have hung the ones that are left in a row all the way up my stairs. Susannah has given them names. Alphabetically. Abbie, Barney, Cindy, Davey. I'm sure she picked the second one for her father, to see if I would flinch at an angel called Barney – I try not to. I think my mother would approve. If I wanted to allow myself the same kinds of belief she had, I would say I hear her giggling as we go up the stairs. But I don't.

7

The Changeling

Hinty minty cutey corn,
Apple seed and apple thorn,
Wire, briar, limber lock,
Three geese in a flock.
One flew east, and one flew west
One flew over the cuckoo's nest.

My mother claimed to believe in a lot of things. Things you say to children. Most of them I knew were nonsense all along. The tree roots hanging down inside the little sandstone cave above the bridge were never an old witch called Grandma Grump. It was always tree roots. The nettles to guard the entrance were simply nettles, not some kind of enchantment.

When we had French toast for breakfast, she would say that her good friend Madame Pamplemousse had flown over from Normandy with it that very morning and landed her helicopter in the back field. I joined in shouting, 'Merci, Madame

Pamplemousse!' out of the kitchen window, claiming to catch sight of the helicopter as it headed back south.

Other things were a grey area. She had a book with photographs of the Cottingley Fairies, beautiful fakery made of cut-out fairies with white flimsy dresses and perfect wings that had fooled quite a few people at the time. When I said, but the whole book is about how they made the little cut-out dollies and propped them up on lolly sticks and made the pictures look real, she said, 'Yes, but just think. If the little girls who played with the fairies wanted people to believe in them, they had to make them look like picture-book fairies in dresses and wings and pretty little faces. The REAL fairies they played with in their gardens might have looked totally different. Really ugly, perhaps, with no clothes on at all. Little brown bellies hanging down over their knees and earlobes sprouting grass.'

She asked for a tree's permission before cutting a branch. Or perhaps that was only elder trees. Or rowan trees. She always saluted single magpies. If you accidentally both said the same word at the same time you had to undo the bad spell by turning around anticlockwise (widdershins she called it), then standing on one leg, putting a finger on the other person's nose and shouting out the name of a poet. Any poet would do. I always shouted Robert Louis Stevenson. She always shouted Ella Wheeler Wilcox, who I never thought was a real person. I thought she was just a funny kind of name to shout out loud. People tell their children all kinds of stories. It's fun. When they grow up and you are still there, you can laugh together about it. But what if your mother disappears into the middle of one of her stories? What if she is taken by the fairies? That was one of her favourites, the story of the changeling.

At the full moon a beautiful child is asleep in her cradle, and the fairies come and steal her away. They take her to their own country, which is tucked inside our world but invisible, and only the fairies know how to move between the two. They leave in the cradle one of their own fairy babies, a changeling child.

The changeling child grows but does not grow strong. It is strangely heavy, dense and unwieldy. It learns to sing but cannot use any other language. Worse than that, the changeling is wilful, mischievous beyond all imagining.

And all the time the mother knows the fairies are watching her, making sure she is kind to the changeling. She daren't punish the child or speak to it sharply, in case the fairies punish her own baby. The changeling is a trial to her, a long test of love that cannot be returned, but she gives it all the love she can, trusting the fairies will do the same for her real baby in return.

There was no happy ending. Any time I asked, 'But what happened next? What happened to her own baby?', my mother would shrug and say, 'No one knows.'

'And the changeling child? What happens to her in the end?'

'Oh, they never thrive. Changelings. They never really grow up.' I was terrified by the changeling story, even before she disappeared.

After she left I wondered, had I been spirited away, or had she? Was I still in the real world, or was this some kind of bad copy? What if my mother was looking everywhere for me, calling my name? What if I could fall backwards out of this poor, faded replica of reality and land in the middle of a bed of spurge, look up and see my mother sitting under the apple tree, threading her needle to sew my name onto school clothes I would never have to wear?

After I had Susannah I understood the changeling story in a different way. I understood the daily miracle when your child wakes and climbs into your arms, still present, still herself. The fever breaks, her tantrum blows over, the sun rises, the medication kicks in, and here she is again, light and strong and determinedly, powerfully herself.

Another thing. It's probably nothing, but every time I try to write down what my mother believed, the file implodes. It disappears into the computer. It falls down behind the radiator, and when I come to staple the pages together it is missing again. I can't tell you how many times I have tried to make a list of what she believed, or what she told me she believed. This is not a complete list. Half of it has gone again. I wanted to tell you about her ghosts, her enchantments and prayers, the bottles hanging above the kitchen door, how the soul can pass when you die into any other living thing, an animal, a tree, and then into a musical instrument cut from the tree. But my attempts keep disappearing. I don't want to sound like my mother here, but I get the feeling she doesn't like me trying to write it down.

From time to time Edward will try to tidy up, and bring me a box of things he thinks belong to me. In among a collection of stuffed animals I swear I had never seen before, he brought me a hardback copy of *Charlotte's Web*. He said he knew the book was important to me, he remembered when I taught myself to read for a second time, home from school with chickenpox, how I had sat in the window seat concentrating so hard on the book to stop myself picking my scabs. By the time the scabs had gone I could read again. Slowly, badly. But I could read.

I remember the soft edges of my paperback copy, the split in the spine from all the handling, the oily spots of calamine lotion on the pages. The one he brought me was pristine. With a hard cover I didn't recognise. I didn't tell him he got me the wrong book, though. Because for some reason my name is written inside the copy he brought me, in writing that looks like mine, in a green ink pen.

I remember *Charlotte's Web* on the window seat. But I was not alone. My mother was there, reading to me, going back over my favourite bits the way I like to, never minding that we'd already read that page. Over and over. I remember her cool hand over mine, moving mine away from the spots on my wrist and those tricky ones nestled inside the soft inner fold of my elbow. Her hands tucked my hair behind my ear, smoothing it away from the line of spots along my eyebrow, the ones that left a line of tiny dots behind. She made up different voices for the characters, a thin scratchy voice for Templeton the rat, a soft, slow, cakey voice for Wilbur, a sort of old-fashioned schoolteacher for Charlotte.

Even though I know she was long gone before I got chickenpox. And I refuse to believe in ghosts. Stubbornly, against the evidence, I refuse to believe in the things she believed in. Even though there would be some comfort in it. Even though the past is folded over and over like puff pastry and my mother, of all people, would understand just how I am wrapped up in its layers and cannot find my way out.

8

What Was Lost in the Long Grass

Green peas, mutton pies,
Tell me where my mother lies.
I'll be there before she dies,
Green peas, mutton pies.

The year I started secondary school we all had to learn how to use an electric sewing machine. Three of the boys in my class were brilliant at it. They were the same boys who sat at the back in everything and threw chewed-up paper at the teachers. A year later they were expelled for breaking all the windows in the chemistry lab. But briefly, at the start of secondary school, their electric sewing machine embroidery was on display in the foyer.

Their ability to control an electric sewing machine was down to the fact that all of them could drive tractors. If you have been driving a tractor with wooden crates tied to the pedals ever since your feet were able to reach halfway, then an electric sewing machine is just another pedal. Easy.

I felt a brief moment of fellow feeling for the tractor drivers and their electric sewing. Because I knew that nothing you learn at home works for you at school. Except by accident. At home I could make bread, sing songs, climb trees, do tricks to make my baby brother laugh when he was crying; I could take important phone messages and read bedtime stories, scoop the tops out of cupcakes and turn them into fairy wings in butter cream; I could part my hair down the back with the hard end of a comb and plait it up for sleeping with no one to help me.

But at school I never knew when to say something and when to shut up, I never knew if I was in week A or week B of the timetable, or what socks you needed for PE this half-term and why they were not the same ones as last time.

I knew the name for the Egyptian household god associated with childbirth, the one with the tail of a crocodile and the body of a lion and the face of a hippopotamus. I could name the tributaries of the Nile. But that stuff is not important. What is important is what kind of colouring pencils you have, and what kind of Tupperware you have for your packed lunch. Washing your own socks is clever at home. But only being able to find odd ones, and one of them being dyed slightly grey, is definitely not clever at school, even though they are both halves of the same thing.

And being stupid at primary school is bad enough, but it is nothing to how bad it is when you get to the high school. There are hardly any girls in the bottom groups, and no one wants to know them. Reading slowly, or reading everything twice just to make sure you get it right, means you cannot keep up with the tasks that the neat girls complete with their unchewed colouring pencils. Reading slowly means you have not got your cooking into the oven on time and it has to go into the bin while the neat girls stow theirs in their special big Tupperware and take it home for supper.

Besides, even if I took mine home it would not be safe for Joe to eat because of his bad skin or for Edward, who turned diabetic after my mother left. Maybe Joe would have had eczema anyway. It can start around that age. But Edward came home early one day because his wife had gone out for the afternoon without telling anyone where she was going, and the next thing he knew he was a widower pissing sugar.

He has injected the reality of her desertion every day of his life since, measured it in insulin and stuck it deep into his stomach. It is a precise and chemical effect that divides his life into before and after. One day it will blind him, and cripple him and then it will kill him, and all of that feels appropriate, proportionate. I felt sorry for myself for forgetting how to read. But there was no point in complaining about it at home. I got off lightly and I knew it.

Life after she left divided into things you could fix, and things you could not fix. My hair, for instance, was fixable. At first I didn't understand why it was rough, and brownish, and stuck to my face. Why the brush didn't help. Then I got nits, and Edward learned about tea tree shampoo and plaits and we found out hair is a fixable thing.

Some things could not be fixed. Shock-induced type 2 diabetes. Chronic eczema. The plates I dropped. The chewed-up home-made jumpers that we shrank in the wash. The kitchen garden. The air in the kitchen: the way the air in the kitchen set like jelly, and you had to be brave to walk into it, leave the radio on very loud, or open the door to the living room and leave children's programmes running on a loop to break up the jelly into moveable chunks you could walk through. The way the edge of everything was muffled, soggy, incomprehensible, distant. The distance never really went away.

And there is no natural law, no easy code to work out which is which, the fixable and the unfixable. That is the trouble. You have to keep trying to fix them all to find out.

Despite my slowness, I still read constantly. It took me longer, so I stayed up later. Night times were never that quiet at our house now. Joe was more bothered by his itches at night, with nothing to distract him, and Edward paced and soothed and put his creams on and read to him. Sometimes I heard the murmur of the story voice or the crying or the sound of the landing cupboard opening when Edward tried cool clean sheets to help settle him. If I got up too we made warm drinks, and I lay on the other side of Edward's bed with Joe lying between us, and held his little hot dry hands gently, and listened to the old stories over and over.

In the morning Edward would be paper-thin from sleeplessness, and I would simply refuse to move. I got up late and missed the school bus and had not brushed my hair or remembered what I was supposed to do that day. So I stayed at home instead. Edward and Joe would already be long gone into town, where Joe went to the workplace nursery at Edward's college.

Some days I set off for the school bus, but then at the last minute I would lose my nerve, hide behind the hedge and watch it leave without me, then let myself in through the dodgy catch on the dining room window. Even if Edward had remembered to lock it, I had an unlocking tool made out of an unravelled coat hanger that I kept under the oil tank.

Once back in the house I made myself the breakfast I had skipped, and went back to bed so I wouldn't need to switch on the heating. I filled my bed with toast crumbs and my mother's books with the covers split open and the pages turned down where I had fallen asleep on them.

The phone rang around nine-thirty when the school office called to ask why I was not in. Sometimes I answered it and pretended to be a childminder or a cleaner. I had a range of funny voices. Well, I thought they were funny. Especially the Scottish ones. I practised rolling the 'r' in Brown, rounding out the vowel.

'Yes, I work for the Brrrroon family. Marianne Brrroon has gone for an X-ray this morning after dropping the iron on her foot, and there is, as usual, a long queue. The underfunding is a scandal!' If they asked to speak to Edward I always offered to pass on a message and said he would be home after six. I knew they would go home before then.

I went back to the books I had read with my mother, over and over, because I already knew the words. Then I read her gardening and cookery books. I traced and retraced her name signed in everything she owned, followed the trail she had left, trying to track her down.

That is when I first started trying to read *Pearl*. My mother's copy of the poem had a plain green cover decorated with a pentangle. I recognised the shape from somewhere. Somewhere important. I knew how to draw one, instinctively, never letting the pencil off the paper. I knew this must be something my mother taught me, but I didn't know where I had seen it before, why she had been teaching me.

Inside was *Sir Gawain and the Green Knight*, then *Pearl*. The *Gawain* section of the book was annotated with vocabulary notes copied from the back of the book, and the section describing Gawain's armour as he dresses to set out on his quest is particularly well scribbled on. Listed down the side of the page are the sets of five that the pentangle represents: his five senses, his five virtues, his five fingers and the five pleasures the holy mother takes in her child. It does not say what the five pleasures might be.

I didn't know that it meant the five mysteries of the rosary. I thought the holy mother had five ways to feel happy with her child. I tried to work out what they would be. I had watched my mother with Joe so I had a fair idea. I knew she had felt him grow rounder and more knobbly inside her all through the winter.

I knew she loved to watch him wriggle his legs, to feed him, to bathe him, to kiss the top of his soft head or the soles of his feet, to make him stripy jumpers he could grow into later, to sing him songs, and rock him and pat him on the back and carry him on her shoulder while he dribbled milk down a square of muslin. The pentangle didn't have enough points for all the pleasures she could take in her child. Perhaps the virgin mother was only allowed five. Which ones would she choose?

The notes thin out after *Gawain*. There are plenty in the first few pages of *Pearl*, but then they fade away. The reason I kept trying to read it was the note she had made in the index. She had circled the word Pearl and drawn an arrow into the margin where she wrote in capitals: CONSOLATIO. I didn't know why she had missed off the last letter. But consolation was what I was looking for. I was ransacking her books for it.

I was secretly collecting clothes from the drawers under her bed and keeping them under my pillow one at a time, trying to preserve the smell of cinnamon-soaked beads she kept in there with them. I was rubbing leaves from the garden into my palm, looking for the perfect spell of mint and pea shoot and fresh onion, and when I pulled nettles instead, dragging the stinging side all the way up the stem between my fingers, I wrapped my hand in dock leaves and believed the stinging was a part of the magic. If I suffered enough I could make her reappear.

Pearl was too hard for me to read. I could manage the first few pages where she had written words in the margins and even drawn little sketches of the herb garden and the grave. At least, it might have been a picture of the herb garden in the poem, or it might be where she had drawn a plan of her own garden, much later. The pencil markings were worn and faded, and had printed themselves onto the opposite side, so the words appeared to be secret incantations in another alphabet. But I persisted, as well as I persisted with anything. I copied out sections into exercise books. I learned how to write the odd curly letters that had disappeared from the language. I had no idea what they meant, what sounds they made.

Her writing in the index promised me consolation. No one else had suggested that was possible. But how could I know: was this a fixable or an unfixable thing? I believed if I could read all the way to the end of the poem, I would be consoled. It didn't matter to me that she might never have finished reading it herself, or that she had probably not opened the book in over a decade, ever since she left college.

It didn't even matter to me that the book had been secondhand when she got it, the name of some other student written in blue ink inside the cover, then crossed out and replaced with her own name before she was married: Margaret Brooke. It didn't occur to me for years that the notes inside might not have been hers at all. I didn't even know if she liked it.

I knew she liked *Sir Gawain and the Green Knight*. She told me the story many times. She always called the chapel on the river the Green Chapel, and it was only years after she died that I found out the real Green Chapel, the one in the story, is about an hour's drive away, and not even a chapel building, more like a green burial mound down a dark path. Or at least I think she told me the story of Sir Gawain. I might have mixed it up with another one of her favourites, the one about the green children.

Once, when some people in the village were digging stone out of the quarry to build their houses, two green children walked out of the earth. A sister and brother. Their clothes were green, and their hair was green, but that's not all. Their skin was green too, and even the whites of their eyes were the palest green.

The children were terrified, and they spoke some language no one understood. They pointed to their mouths to show they were hungry but when the villagers offered them bread and cheese and apples they wouldn't eat them.

So the villagers stopped their digging and took the children to the man who owned all the land thereabouts, a man who had travelled and knew different languages. The landowner tried all the languages he could think of, but he couldn't talk to them either. He was a kind man, and offered them everything he could think of to eat, and when someone offered them green beans they ate them.

The children stayed with him, and gradually they began to eat more things, and their green colour started to fade, and soon they learned the language of the people around them. Even after their skin changed colour they had green eyes like cats, and their hair stayed the colour of wet straw.

The children said they had wandered into a cave and when they came out, they couldn't find their way back. They said everyone was green where they came from. The villagers helped them to look for the way back, but no one could find it. So the children stayed.

The little boy died, and they buried him near where he had been found, hoping his ghost would know the way home. The girl grew up and married, and had half-green children of her own, but she never stopped looking for the way back to her first home, and she never found it.

Or that is the story I found when I looked it up. In the version my mother told me, both the children were too homesick, and they both died. I must have remembered it wrongly. Or I might have preferred the idea of the children staying together. I didn't like the idea of the sister living on in a strange land without her brother. I might have asked my mother for a different ending, or I might have changed it for myself after she left.

9

Lines of Enquiry

Eaper Weeper Chimney Sweeper
Had a wife but couldn't keep her.
He put her in a pumpkin shell
And there he kept her very well.

Among my mother's books was a little Victorian fortune-telling book called *The Ladies' Oracle*. You can ask any of the questions it gives, and then you close your eyes and concentrate on your question, and point to a page of symbols. Then you follow the symbols back to the page with your answer. The questions are all things like 'Does he who I think of think also of me?' and the answer is usually a variant on 'Maybe. Wait and see.'

Many of the questions relate to the danger of scandal. There are plenty of questions like 'If my fault is discovered, will it be pardoned?' and 'What must I do to prevent their discovering that which I wish to conceal?' and then, for those wavering on the brink of non-virtuous behaviour, 'Ought I to break it off or yield?' For more definite questions like 'Will I have any children?' I once got 'One charming one, and several detestable ones.' Thanks.

Despite its ridiculous questions and worse answers, I consulted *The Ladies' Oracle* regularly throughout my teens and totally disregarded all of its advice. I think that is what it's for. And although I didn't look anything like the Victorian girl on the cover hiding behind a fan, my concerns were not really that different. Does she love me? Will we be happy? Does anyone know my secret? Will she still love me if she finds out?

I used to think I was good at question-and-answer games. I played a lot of them with my mother and she taught me there were lots of different ways to answer a question correctly. The first time a police officer said to me, 'I need to ask you some questions', I felt a moment of relief. If the whole thing could be solved, sorted and returned to normal by means of questions and answers I was sure we would do so in a few hours.

But it turned out I was no good at these questions at all. There was something wrong with my answers. I tried again. I said a different thing. I kept looking up at their faces, for a sign that I had got it right: I was watching for their expressions to change from puzzled and embarrassed into impressed and delighted, and then everything would be alright. Nothing I knew about questions and answers helped me now. Because the police only had one right answer, and I didn't know what it was. The more ways I tried to answer it, the more trouble I was in.

They would flick back through the little notebooks, folding the pages back to yesterday, the day before, checking what I said last time. It never matched up. Yesterday's answer had not worked. She was still lost. So I tried another one. I looked about me and picked up random objects, explaining, with increasingly imaginative storylines, how they were clues. They gave up asking me questions and I knew I had failed.

They asked a lot of questions about where she might leave a note. Where would she leave a message? Sometimes people leave a message where they go into the water. But it was raining, and there was nowhere safe to leave an envelope. Perhaps at the old chapel? There were some of our old jam jars there but all we found in them were rotting ribbons from old bunches of flowers, ends of candles, spiders, moss.

Perhaps it floated away on the swollen river to catch on some distant reed bed or bank, and washed away to nothing. Perhaps it was in her pocket. But most probably we never found a note because she did not write one for us. And without a note we cannot prove that she ever meant to disappear.

There were also a lot of questions about what she had taken with her when she left. A coat might mean she intended to travel some distance. A pair of wellies might indicate taking the flooded footpath or the short cut over the field. Money means intention to use transport. Make-up might mean she was meeting someone. Smart clothes. A suitcase suggests she is going to stay with someone. A map would show she had a destination in mind.

But it is very difficult to work out what a person might have taken with them. You have to know exactly how many of everything they have to start with, and then work out exactly how many are left behind. We didn't know either.

Edward tried to keep their questions from me, but he couldn't. I was one of the last people to see her, so they had to ask me things. And I was always there, trying to keep Joe occupied while they interviewed Edward, listening intently through the open kitchen door, peering sleepless through the banisters after dark and tuning into his answers or his late-night phone calls to friends and colleagues. What was she hiding? Who could she have been meeting?

They especially liked that one. Every time new people come along and try to solve the case, they come back to that one. It's their favourite line of enquiry. Personally, I eliminated it years ago, but the detectives liked it so much I feel I ought to include it. I leave it to you if you can dismiss it as easily as I did.

In the 1970s the countryside was full of overeducated women from the cities who believed in a return to nature. They wanted their children to grow up riding their bikes down muddy lanes and building dens in the hedges. They wanted to grow their own vegetables and bottle their own fruit and make their own clothes. But there's a problem with that: doesn't it mean they are back in the kitchen with no means to earn their own living? Haven't they just slid back a generation and handed the keys to the car and the family chequebook over to their husbands? My mother grew up over a grocer's shop where my grandmother worked twelve-hour days alongside her husband and had the same access to money that he did. She spent her early years on the floor of the shop and my grandmother fed her behind the counter until she was old enough to stack tins and carry things around. She did her homework on a little shelf her dad built to slide out from under one side of the till so she could still mind the shop while she took her A levels, and she went to the nearest university so she could still help in the shop all weekend.

When my grandmother died the business fell to pieces along with her husband, and neither lasted a year without her. After the debts and funeral were paid off, the lease on the shop was ended. My mother was a student then. She moved into halls of residence for her last year, and married Edward a week after graduation. He was her history lecturer.

She came from a long line of working women, women who never questioned their right to earn money. They simply had to. Childcare was a luxury that rich people paid for. Children had to join in, shut up and keep out of the way. My mother had no model to follow when she moved to a crumbling old house in the country and tried to grow her own food and educate her own children. She was making it up as she went along.

There was no public transport. No internet. She had no income, no car. She didn't know anyone there, and because I never went to school, she never met the other parents.

One thing that happened when all these educated and idealistic women were suddenly cut off from the world of work and money and power is that they had affairs. In the countryside that meant meeting in barns and sheltered corners of fields. It meant people finding out. Nothing stays secret in a village.

I don't think she was meeting anyone that day. If she had planned to go out at all, she would have asked Mrs Wynne to stay longer and babysit. She would have left a bottle made up, and a list of feed times. She would have taken her good shoes and a coat. Money, a bag. She would have arranged for a lift from the end of the lane, and set out in wellies, carrying an umbrella in one hand, a bag with her shoes in the other.

We know that is what she would have done, because, years before, when she went to meet someone, that is what she did. So everyone in the village knew about it. And now I do too. The man she went to meet owned some fields on the other side of the village. When she asked at the village shop if anyone might come and help her with her garden, give her advice, or maybe sell her some manure for her new vegetable beds, the woman in the shop said she'd get Stan to call round.

One morning she went out to her garden in her dressing gown before breakfast, to drink her tea and let her chickens out, and he was there, leaning on her garden fork and rolling himself a cigarette. He told her she was digging in all the wrong places, that most of the apple trees were beyond pruning, and besides were only good for cooking, and he took two sugars and plenty of milk.

Stan always looks out of place indoors. He has the village manner of talking quite slowly, and finishing a sentence by trailing off and giving a kind of shrug, or a glance to the horizon as if to say 'You know what I mean, I won't bother you further.' I have no idea how much of the gossip about him and my mother was true. All I have known of him myself is kindness.

After my mother disappeared he left piles of firewood in our yard, free of charge, said he had some trees down anyway, and at least we could be warm. He came out at odd hours and mended our roof, or held bits of the barn together in bad weather. He dug out the ditches alongside our lane to stop it flooding. When the garden had run wild he came with a ride-on mower and tidied it all down to a rough, patchy lawn that at least we could live with. He went round under the ancient cooking-apple trees before he did the mowing and piled all the rotten waspy apples into hessian sacks.

He never came into the house. If invited, he would half shrug and indicate his half-smoked cigarette as an excuse. He would knock on the kitchen window and say, 'Two sugars, good ones now. Plenty of milk.' He always left the mug out in the garden somewhere.

I have never written off his years of kindness as proof of a guilty conscience. He chose to be our friend when most people wanted nothing to do with us. If the police came and questioned him, over and over, down the years, upsetting his wife each time, bringing it all back, going over and over the details, he did not hold it against us. He kept on replacing slates on our roof and taking out rotten slats in the barn door and digging black silt out of our ditches and carrying wood for our fire.

He is a comfortable man, easy to be with. He does not talk a lot. If they had an affair, who am I to blame them? I have not managed to stay married, as they both did. I have hardly managed to stay anywhere near married. Isolated, adrift, would I be proof against a kind man, a man who had a soft spot for me? Probably not.

I am not telling you the whole story. They took her journals and notebooks. They read them all. They took photographs of those pages that dealt with the affair. She wrote poems about it. Embarrassing love poems. They showed them to my father. They did it on purpose, to watch his reaction, to gauge if he was murderous. Was he a wronged husband, out for revenge?

Did he have a dangerous temper? And if he showed nothing and remained calm, was he heartless? Did he keep her locked away at the end of the lane with no money and no car so he could dominate her? Why did the child not go to school? Was she hiding bruises? What were they keeping secret?

All those journals and love poems are from before I was born. So I cannot tell you anything about how my father and the rest of the village found them out, how my parents managed to repair their marriage and continue together, happily, I think. I don't know if the gossip hurt her, kept her from making friends. When I knew them my parents were so close they didn't seem to need anyone else. They half finished jokes and raised their eyebrows together to mean any number of things. They read the same books.

I know the next question, so I'll put it to bed now. This is not going to be the sort of story where I find out I am not really my father's daughter, and blame this for my bad behaviour or difficult relationships with men. Yes, my mother almost certainly had an affair some time before I was born. But you don't grow up with freckles like this and harbour doubts about your parentage. I look exactly like Joe. And at least half like my father. More than that, I have never thought it mattered. Why would I even care? It is hard enough, and good enough, to be the daughter of my real parents. They are more than enough, in every sense.

I overheard Edward say something about that time to one of his friends. He had taken the phone into the garden, and as he walked past the open window I heard him say, 'It's not like I was the perfect husband either, at the time. You know.' So I guess that means he was having affairs as well. Or one, at least. At least one that his friend knew about.

There's a word for it, I know. Minimising. It is easier than total denial. Denial requires the ability to override your primary data. Minimising merely requires you to see it, hear it, and then move it into a less critical category. That is what I do with the evidence of my parents' affairs. I accept they happened. I choose to believe it is not the answer to everything.

In the village we all minimise. It's a way of life. If someone commits a crime, we say, 'Oh, but it's only Jonesy, he didn't mean it.' Even though I have left the village far behind me now, I have kept that habit. I minimise. It is a dangerous thing to do. I ought to know better. It belongs in my parents' generation, really. It's dated. People their age used to say, 'Don't exaggerate.' Especially to children. Don't be so dramatic. Really, Marianne. Hate is too strong a word. But it wasn't.

I hated school. I hated school uniform socks. I hated my teachers. I hated my classmates. I hated my hair. I hated the special reading teacher who visited every term. I hated their letters home in their specially minimised language. Marianne is taking a while to settle into school routine. Marianne has some ability but she needs to settle into good school habits to make the most of it. Marianne can be difficult at times.

If hate is too strong a word, how about love? Did my mother love Stan? She said she did in her poems. Did my father forgive her? Or is forgiveness too strong a word as well?

10

A Spoon Called Geoffrey

House to let, enquire within,
Men turned out for drinking gin,
Smoking tobacco, pinching snuff,
Don't you think that's quite enough?

I didn't protest much about moving house at first. Edward sat me down and basically explained the existence of money in the world, and it was news to me. I could see the house we were living in needed some help to stop it leaking and wobbling and being cold. Now I found out about the cost of nursery care and transport and a thing called debts. I found out that those annoying extra teachers I ignored or was rude to were costing a lot of this thing called money.

I was a teenager then, just, and I thought moving to a town would mean more freedom, more places to go. I heard the word 'town house' and I imagined a tall, elegant terrace with attics and cellars and curved stone steps up to the door. I wondered if I would get the top floor to myself.

Besides, our own house had become such a ramshackle, hopeless maze of guilt-ridden corners, the garden a tangled forest of bramble. The track to the road had become dangerously pot-holed, and this meant either leaving the car in the gateway on the road and walking up in our wellies or else risking the exhaust and various other things that lived on the bottom of the car and which I did not even know the names for. But these things also cost money.

Joe was due to leave the nursery at the college where Edward worked, and which was open from eight in the morning to six at night. Schools were not. If Joe went to the village school there would be extra childminders in the morning and the evening. Schools back then didn't offer much in the way of extended hours. If we moved to the town and lived near the university, Joe could still go to the same nursery for breakfast and they walked the older children to and from school in a little crocodile. He would stay with the same children he had been with all along.

I hadn't really considered Joe having friends. Surely they spent the day chewing plasticine and weeing on the floor and biting each other? I realised he had a whole other world, the world he and Edward shared in long car trips morning and evening, one I only saw in discarded snack wrappers and mouldy sippy-cups of gone-off milk and story tapes and piles of rubbish artwork and junk models he brought home with him and which never got beyond the back seat of the car. Now this other world that I had totally ignored was going to take precedence over my own.

Then there was the issue of Joe's allergies. The school

in town already had a child there with a similar range of allergic reactions, and they were willing to make all the special arrangements. And Edward and the hospital were five minutes away in case of emergencies.

Edward reasoned with me that I hardly ever attended school anyway, so it wouldn't really matter if I went somewhere else. I might even prefer it. He had a chart that my school had sent him, showing my attendance, or lack of it. It showed green for those days or parts of the days where I had been in lessons and red for an absence that he had not authorised. Orange was for the parts of days he had arranged private lessons for me.

My chart looked like a fireworks display. It was supposed to look like a farm. I was surprised to find they had been keeping track at all. They hardly ever spoke to me about it. This was my first experience of realising too late that people whose job it is to keep a tally of things are generally keeping a tally of things.

Then there was the problem of selling the old house. We had to keep it tidy for people to look around and mostly they came in the school day with the agents, when I was not supposed to be there. But I was. So I ended up hiding in corners of the barn or in the garden, trying to guess if they liked it, or if I liked them enough to let them have it. August came and still no one wanted to buy it. Joe had a place at the school in town. So did I, although I had refused to go and visit it. So now what?

Edward sat me down again and explained something called a Bridging Loan which was a lot more debt, but we could move into a house he had found near to work. The owners had gone into a nursing home and did not need their furniture any more, so we could move right in and leave the old house as it was until someone bought it. The Bridging Loan would mean we had to wait to do things to the new house like get different carpets or a nicer bathroom, but these things could wait, and the start of school could not.

I said, 'Since when did we even care about the start of stupid school?' and he said, 'Since we needed free childcare provided by the state for working parents, which is basically the point of it.' And there I was thinking it had something to do with education. But that was before I knew about money.

I went into a too-late and totally unhelpful sulk about it, and refused to help pack up even my own things. Edward left the agent's details for the New House on the kitchen table and put Post-it notes on it saying things like 'Marianne's Room?' or 'Piano can go here?' or 'Watching TV together in this room?' I spilled sugary tea over them and stuck the fold of glossy paper together so we couldn't see the photographs of the rooms inside. Which was probably just as well.

I did agree to go and see it for myself about a week before we moved in. We pulled into a brick-paved driveway in front of a squat red semi-detached house with a huge ugly bay window on the ground floor with mottled frosted coloured glass in the tops of the windows. I refused to get out of the car. But after a while I was so desperate for a wee I had to go and ring the bell to get Edward to let me in to use the toilet.

Along the curve of the driveway were orange plastic flower pots full of dead stalks. The previous owners had tacked a porch over the front door with handrails along the walls. The bell played a desperately sad little tinny tune. The carpet in the porch, hall and stairs was a thin nylon geometric pattern that managed to hit the edge of each tread on a slightly different part of the pattern so your eyes went squinty and you felt a bit sick. Everywhere smelled wrong. Like water tastes wrong away from home. Not bad, just wrong.

Joe was running in and out of the two living rooms, one front and one back, both square and high and matching in size and ugliness. He could not reach the doorknobs, which were high up and made of some kind of dull brittle plastic. There were ceramic plates with pink and purple flowers painted on them on the doors.

I set off up the stairs in search of a toilet. When I found it, in a little room all of its own, it had a kind of scaffolding around it for old people to get on and off the seat. The toilet-roll holder was pink plastic.

I found my bedroom at the front of the house. There was a tiny pale-brown tiled fireplace surrounded by huge white plastic cupboard doors. There were twin beds with quilted yellow coverlets. The cupboards were full of different coloured sheets, the shelves labelled neatly with masking tape: front bedroom, back bedroom, new bedroom.

The new bedroom was an extension over the kitchen, and this was for Joe. This was the only room that had been emptied, because of Joe's allergies, and a laminate floor fitted to avoid any dust or fibres. Edward had ordered Joe a huge complicated bed with a little ladder and a playhouse under it, and he spent the rest of the day building this, with Joe helping him by passing him the wrong tools and running off with important pieces of wood.

I spent the time taking all the bedding off the beds and out of the cupboards in my room and piling it up in the hallway. There were extra frilly bits that hung down over the legs of the beds. Every armful smelled of someone else's house. I took down the flowery curtains, and the tiny plastic hooks fell to pieces in my hands and the pieces fell into the yellow shagpile carpet under the window. Behind the first curtains were equally flowery nets, acres and acres of sharp, lemon-smelling cloth.

When I had piled them all in the hallway Edward said, 'You might need those nets at the front. With the street lamps, and not wanting people to see in.' I had never heard of curtains to stop people looking in. Outside our windows in the Old House were cows and hedges and the occasional bat or owl. Curtains were to keep the warmth in when you had lit the fire or to stop the draught coming in through the kitchen door.

When we all got hungry we walked along the road past countless other red brick houses with bay windows, in sets of two with identical gravel driveways, until we found a little row of shops where we got fish and chips and a bottle of milk. The walk felt to me like a very long way, because I was used to seeing houses as landmarks, and there were so many of them.

When we looked in the kitchen for something for Joe to drink out of, we found some tiny glasses with old-fashioned cartoon characters on them. Edward said they were probably collector's items. We could see they had belonged to the children in the house, a long time ago when there were children in the house. There were other treasures. We found a child's spoon with an elephant on the top, and the name Geoffrey engraved along it.

'Bargain,' I said. 'Not only do we get to keep their purple and green flowery bed sheets, but we get a spoon called Geoffrey.'

Edward said, 'Don't be silly. It's obvious it's the elephant who's called Geoffrey.' I knew that now we were making jokes about the cutlery there was no going back on it. I was going to have to ADJUST.

We always call it the New House. For twenty-seven years we've called it the New House. As long as it's the New House we can be excused the sorry attempts we have made at taming it, laying claim to it, or making it feel like our home. If it ever became simply the House we might have to move in properly, take the last owners' armchairs out of the back sitting room and strip the terrible wallpaper off the front room instead of simply building more and more bookshelves over the top of it.

I was not the only one who found it hard to adjust. Edward didn't say he missed the Old House. He didn't have to. He constantly drove past the New House by accident when he was coming home from work, then had to turn around at the end of the road and come back. Then the turn into the drive was too sharp from that side of the road, so he would come in at the wrong angle and scrape the paint off one side of the car against the gatepost. He never even tried to get it repaired.

He would look in a cupboard for something that wasn't there, and shut it slightly harder than he had to. Or I would find him staring out of the kitchen window at nothing, as if he was looking for some trace of the view from the last one. I saw him stir odd piles of mess on the windowsills in a dismissive, desultory way, accusing them of having nothing to do with him.

At the weekend he would say, 'I thought we'd better pop over to the old place, make sure she isn't falling down without us,' and he'd try to say it in an upbeat way which fooled no one at all. I hadn't even known until then he called the Old House She.

The New House was definitely a He. What's more, He could sense we didn't really like him, and while we were away at the weekends He pulled tricks on us. When we got back on Sunday night He refused to let our key work in the door until it snapped and we had to break a window in the downstairs toilet for me to climb in and pull myself inside by grabbing the sides of the toilet bowl upside down.

The New House laughed at us. No matter what we carried into the hall it reverted to its original smell of talcum powder and old raincoats. Tiles slid down its roof and crashed onto the driveway right next to the car as we arrived, a warning shot. The inside doors swelled and jammed and refused to let us into certain rooms. The electric fire in the front room burst into flames the first time we switched it on. The plumbing had a thing called a Water Hammer, which meant if you flushed the toilet at night it set up a full thirty minutes of banging noise that woke not only us but the people next door, who claimed it had never happened with the previous occupants. One Sunday night we stepped inside and barely had time to register the fact that our feet were wet before we switched on the hall light and blew all the fuses. The water tank had split and emptied itself into the hall via the light fitting.

We had no money to mend any of these things. The front door had a broken key in it for the best part of a year. We simply came round the back. The hall ceiling dried out, leaving a dark orange stain, and the light never worked again. We used the one on the landing instead. We closed off the water tank system and used the electric shower, which meant carrying a bowl of water down the stairs every time you had to do the washing up. The stairs were soon stained and blotchy from all the spills of water. Edward said, never mind, we'll replace this carpet as soon as there's some money.

We patched the broken window in the downstairs loo with a piece of wood, so I found it easy to slip in and out whenever I chose to come home early from school. Usually around 9.30 a.m. I got used to the slide in through the top window, the grab around the smelly toilet, the slither and bump as I hit the floor, knocking aside Joe's special step and plastic seat.

And soon we discovered that a lot of the things that depressed us about our life in the Old House followed us into the New House. We were oppressed by Things. The thing-ness of all the Things. Last week's swimming lesson bag gone smelly under the coat hooks. Lost letters from school. Missing pieces of board games, hideous free toys in plastic bags, the kitchen side covered in unopened letters from the bank and random half-finished drawings and old shopping lists we forgot to take shopping with us, Lego bricks and school shirts with missing buttons and dead plants and clothes pegs with one side missing and seed packets we would never sow and plastic beakers half-full of soil which Joe had planted something in at school and which we never watered. Things didn't make sense to us any more. The senselessness of them hemmed us in, drove us from room to room looking for refuge.

At the New House there was the tide of new Things we dragged in our wake, piled on top of the accumulated Things of some other defunct family. At the back of the cupboard, where none of the non-spill beaker tops matched any of the bottoms and the mugs all had a chip or a missing handle, there were souvenirs from places we had never been, tiny ceramic pots with shiny lids for doing something weird with eggs, special spoons for marmalade that had enamel oranges on the tops of their handles and badly made ashtrays painted to look like ladybirds from a time when children made ashtrays in school pottery classes.

Under the sink we found half-empty jars labelled tortoise food filled with mouldy dog biscuits. We found orange glass vases and birdseed that had got wet and grown a little farm around the outlet pipe. In the cutlery drawer were several contraptions for opening jars when your hands are too old to grip, and assorted half-packets of paper napkins carrying the scent of other people's Christmases and other people's children's parties.

I tried a few times to run away to the Old House instead of going to school. I would get as far as avoiding the school bus, head back to the New House, climb in, and think, this is stupid: I'm going home. I knew the Old House was empty. I thought if I set up camp there and flat out refused to leave then Edward would have to give up on the stupid New House and bring Joe back.

But getting to the Old House with nothing but dinner money was difficult. I could sneak onto the stopping train north through Shropshire and dodge the ticket inspectors by getting off and on, waiting on a series of empty platforms on the edge of tiny villages, but at the end of the line I was still a long slow bus ride from the village, and there were hardly any buses.

I did get all the way there twice, but the second time Edward came to fetch me he said he was taking the cost of the petrol out of the next two weeks' dinner money and he would be making me sandwiches for school instead. He also said it was very disruptive of Joe's routine to have to spend the evening driving to and fro instead of having a quiet supper of fish fingers and doing his reading book. The next time he would ask the police to fetch me back instead. If they could be bothered.

On the drive home he told me how he had run away to that house himself, when he was about my age. He was at boarding school, which he hated, and he knew his parents would send him straight back if he made his way home, so instead he would try to get to Great-Uncle Matthew's. There were no buses at all then, so he walked most of the way. Sometimes it took him days. He packed supplies for the journey by saving food from his plate at school teatime, and set off with a package of semi-stale bread and margarine wrapped in brown paper.

Uncle Matthew usually let him stay at least a few days before sending him back. All in all he got about a week off every time he did it, if you added up the time taken walking there, then the delay and an exchange of letters, which he said made it well worth the blisters from walking, the hunger along the way, and the caning he got on his return. It was one of the reasons he loved the Old House so much. It had always been a place of safety.

I don't know how either of us could bear to leave the place. I guess we thought our hearts were already broken. What more damage could it do? But it did. Losing the place where my mother had lived and been happy was like losing her all over again. The gradual collapse of the Old House without us, its descent into cold and chaos, was a physical loss that brought us both to our knees.

For Edward it was probably worse, as he lost his childhood

there as well, and because of the Money. Having two houses falling down around him at the same time as interest rates went through the roof and the Bridging Loan weighed down on him turned the last of his hair white, curved his shoulders, turned him into an old man. Every new teacher Joe had assumed it was his grandfather coming to parents' evening.

Joe calls it the New House too, but claims not to remember living anywhere else. He is still friends with some of those children from nursery, the ones who belong to Edward's colleagues. It was thanks to him and his extensive list of allergies that we stripped all the horrific carpets and found perfect wooden flooring all through the ground floor, preserved by the layers of nylon patterns.

We have never managed to lay claim to the kitchen. How can a kitchen be cold? It doesn't seem to matter what we cook in it, the room stays echoey and damp, and strangely never smells of food, unless you count lemons. It does smell of lemons. By the time we get food to the table we feel too chilly to sit around in there and eat it, and we end up carrying trays into the back sitting room to our un-favourite chairs and the big brown box of a gas fire.

Now we are both older Edward and I can talk freely about the Old House, what it meant to us, what it meant to lose it. We can talk about it for hours. Watching bats fly in and out of the barn. The long, battered kitchen table with its piles of jigsaw pieces and the old brown teapot in the middle. The warm colour of the garden wall in the late afternoon. The knobbly old apple trees bending their branches to the ground, heavy with huge fruit. The stone floors and worn-down treads of the stairs. The tall arched window on the landing.

And there are the things we can't talk about. The sound of my mother singing along to the radio in the morning. The smell of bread proving. Gleanings from the herb garden gathered in tall handfuls stuck into jugs, the smell of the fire smoking as it started up in the evening, the sweet cedar of her knitting box that made its way into the very fabric of all our jumpers. The smell of clean earth on her hands, of mint and lavender. Her soft, croaky, wheezy laughter, her love of terrible knock-knock jokes, her hair pulled back and twisted on the top of her head, pale brown wispy strands falling over her face and tucked behind her ears.

We can even say now it was a mistake, a failure of imagination, a deep regret that we didn't hang on to the house. At the time it was resigned realism. It's not possible to live a long way from work in the middle of nowhere in an old house that needs a lot of looking after with a young family unless you have a partner at home with the children.

Now we can think of other things we could have done instead, now that we are no longer too exhausted and miserable to think of other solutions. We could have rented in town for a while, or paid for a full-time nanny or au pair, or sold the barn and the land, or sold all of it but kept a corner of the garden for ourselves to build a new house. But we didn't. It's very hard to think of good ideas when you are sad. Later, when you are less sad, the ideas look obvious, but you need an imagination, or something else. You need to believe that what you do matters. Our every step seemed to be telling us to go back. Every inanimate object told us we had missed our way, pushed our noses back to the scent of home, but like the stubborn horse in the adage, we would not drink, would not let our instincts take us the way they longed to go. The Old House and the New House joined forces against us, trying to push us back where we belonged, pulling us back, locking us out, but we didn't go.

We are usually in the back sitting room of the New House having these conversations. We are sitting on the same wooden-armed chairs that were there when we arrived. They had stretchy beige nylon covers on them at first, and when these covers wore through we found beneath them the original tufted coarse stripes like the seats in a train. We put blankets over them to stop them prickling our legs, but the blankets always fall down. When we first saw them we said, we'll get rid of all this stuff. But we never did.

From time to time I promise to sew some better covers that don't fall down, but I haven't got round to it yet, or some visitor will tell us they are worth a fortune, that hardly anyone held on to sixties stuff like that when it became unfashionable, and my god, are those really the original fabric? What a gold mine! And we shrug, and keep sitting on them and complaining that they prickle, and pretending they are nothing to do with us after twenty-seven years.

11
Twiglets

Made ya look
Made ya stare
Made the barber
Cut ya hair

Cut it long
Cut it short
Cut it with
A knife and fork

I haven't told you about the gravestone. I've been putting it off. Because if I tell you about the marker stone I have to tell you about Emily. And then I'll have to tell you about Emily's mother. And the baby. And the fire. And all of that is clogged up with shame. My shame, and Edward's too. Shame is the black sticky stuff that fills the pipes under your sink. It backs up all your worst dirt and leaves it clinging to the sides of the sink for everyone to see. There's no way round it. The water won't run clear until you've dug out every bit of it. And I want the water to run clear. I want to see right through it.

Emily was my girlfriend when I was fifteen. She was older, eighteen, and it felt like a big difference. Emily went to college, not school, and was allowed to wear whatever she liked all day long. Which in her case was a mixture of very expensive and very broken black and grey layers, like cobwebs. Crucially, for me, she had left home, and refused to acknowledge either of her parents. If I asked about them, she said, 'Oh them!'

Edward was not fooled. He said, 'Who do you think pays for that flat of hers?' Edward knew more about her than I did, in a way, because her mother was his head of department, but all the time I was with her I managed to avoid thinking about that. I met her at a garden party at her parents' house. It rained, and all the history department and their partners and children ran into the three massive sitting rooms and crowded in and out of the giant kitchen, collecting drinks and food from a marbletopped counter in the middle of the room. Everyone except me.

I ran into one of their wooden summer houses and played on a running machine. Emily was sitting cross-legged in the middle of a bright yellow yoga mat, smoking a huge joint. She handed it over to me and said, 'I know who you are. You're the one with the suspicious death. The girl who forgot how to read.' I set the running machine to uphill and kept hold of her joint. She said, 'What I want to know is, if you forgot how to read, what else did you forget?'

It's a good question. But there was no way I could answer it. So I said, 'If you can't read very well, you have to have an excellent memory. Think about it.' Then she turned off the running machine at the wall, and I skidded to a stop, and she kissed me. I was just about to ask her how she knew about the reading, which I thought only Edward and I knew about, but as I opened my mouth to ask her, she kissed me again. And I wondered if that was why I had opened my mouth. Or if it had looked like that.

She tasted of weed and red wine and Twiglets. I thought she must have taken some food from the party table. But later, when I was kissing her most days, I realised the slightly peppery Twiglet tang was just her own taste. I said, 'You taste of Twiglets,' and she said, 'Classy! You taste of jelly babies.' It was probably the weed, but we both found this very funny.

She pulled her stringy vest top over her head, and said, 'How about here? What snack food do I taste of here?' And I tested out the space just under the bony wings of her clavicles, left and right. Ready salted. And then I pulled back the next layer of strappy underwear, and the next, and tasted orange peel and vanilla cake on her stomach and digestive biscuits on the inside of her thighs and Twiglets and red wine between her legs. I tasted of lemon peel and white wine. Apparently.

She said, did I have any lip gloss in my bag, because all her stuff was in the house. I handed over a tiny tin of cocoa butter and we rubbed the clean smell of it over our hands and between our legs. Emily liked watching. She had very big green eyes, magnified by her round black-rimmed glasses. Everything else about her was tiny.

She was barely five feet tall, with size three feet. Her skin was sallow, almost yellowish in winter, and her eyebrows were dark brown. You couldn't tell what colour her hair had been, because it was dyed about six different ways. Taking off all her layers of clothes made her smaller and smaller and smaller until I was left with this tiny dark creature in a nest of unpeeled clothing. I felt like a huge pale blob beside her, as if undressing me made me bigger and bigger, loosening all the layers that had held me in.

We smoked another joint and put our clothes back on, the button on my jeans sticky with cocoa butter and salty fingers, the edges of all our clothes smudged and shiny with sex. It had stopped raining by now, and we had missed most of the food. People were coming out into the garden again to play badminton on the lawn. Emily said I had better go back to the house before anyone got suspicious. She didn't come with me. Suspicious was one of her favourite words. And Edward was one of her favourite suspicions.

I can see now, everything about her meant she was rich. Rich enough to take four years to complete a two-year college course if she liked. Rich enough to live in a flat of her own and spend her money on whatever she fancied. Rich enough to have a full set of gym equipment in one of her mother's summer houses. Rich enough to have a supply of dope in her pocket. Rich enough for none of it to matter.

At the weekends she worked in a café, or she said she did. It belonged to a friend of her mother's, and I'm not sure how often she actually turned up. She said I could go there and meet her if I wanted. So I sat in the café making a drink last an hour, hoping she might turn up for work, hoping she might be free to come and sit with me for a while. Occasionally she would.

I could tell Edward didn't want me near her, and this made me curious. He didn't say a lot. But he looked panicked when

I said I'd met her in the summer house. Why didn't she come back to the house with me? What had she said? He said he'd met her a few times, years before, when her mother first joined the department, that she'd always been difficult. Difficult how, I wanted to know. She had been the very opposite with me.

Well, he said, she was probably just protective of her mother, liked to keep her to herself. Who would she be protecting her from? I didn't get it. I said, well, maybe she's changed. Grown up. Yes, yes, he agreed, she must be eighteen by now, and they all seem so much more settled. All? Who did he mean? They certainly looked settled from the outside, with their badminton-sized lawns and marble kitchen and gym equipment and fancy Twiglets. Twiglets? he said. Did I miss Twiglets? I haven't seen them in years. What were we talking about?

Emily gave up pretending to work at her mother's friend's café and started checking coats at a nightclub instead. She let me in the fire door behind the cloakroom in the basement, and we stayed up all night kissing and going through the pockets of all the coats and sharing what we found. We didn't take off any clothes in case someone arrived needing something, and I had to keep ducking back behind the racks if the owners came along, so we spent the entire night in a state of heightened excitement, pushing oily fingers into too-tight jeans, leaving bite marks just inside the neckline of our T-shirts. On rainy nights we would kiss in a fog of steamy wool, the smell of aftershave lifting off the damp denim jackets and the soft mouldy smell of weed rising out of rained-on parkas.

Edward tried again to warn me about her. He said there were all kinds of reasons she was interested in me. Reasons that were not to do with me. Or her. I thought he was talking about the weed.

Besides, I wasn't ready to listen to anything he said about her. I loved her strange layers of differently black clothes, her hair shaved on one side of her head and multicoloured on the other. I liked to rub the shaved side of her head and feel the ripple of soft flesh with its tiny prickles. I liked to help her make extra piercings along her ear lobes. I loved her long thin menthol cigarettes and strange cocktails of vodka and anything else she could find. I loved her collection of vintage hats that she kept on nails, covering a whole wall of her studio flat.

I loved the smoky smell of her, the room she lived in, all alone, with its piles of books she had inherited from the previous tenant and which she used to prop open the shower door, or which she stacked up in a rough rectangle to use as a coffee table. I loved the wall behind her bed where she had written in sharpie any quotation she liked, from the Beatles or more likely the Doors, or Gandhi, or anyone else she felt like adding.

I was allowed to add quotations to the wall if I lay in the bed with her. I copied out all of Philip Larkin's 'This Be the Verse' but she said it was too long. I was taking up too much wall. I thought if I was her girlfriend, I ought to be allowed plenty of wall. So I wrote 'Jesus wept' – the shortest verse in the Bible. She said, 'Okay, you can stop now.' She had lost interest already. That was always happening.

She liked me to come round in my school uniform, straight off the wrong bus, so she could take it all off. One time after she had taken all my clothes off she cut off my hair as well. And shaved my head smooth as an egg.

'Now you are properly naked,' she said. 'Let's see how your liberal daddy takes to your new look!' It was a kind of dare. A deliberate provocation. Edward laughed and said, 'Hair grows back, sweetie.' When something really bad has happened in your family, you learn not to be worried about stuff like how short your daughter's hair is.

The school, on the other hand, got very over-excited about the lack of hair. It was the opportunity they had been looking for to expel me. Truancy I already had down to a fine art. Days spent naked on Emily's rented bed writing poetry in illegal ink on the rented wall hadn't helped my attendance record. And now baldness. There was no specific school rule against shaving your head. So they made one up. Especially for me. I was told to wear a hat until it grew back to an 'acceptable length'. Edward asked how many millimetres was acceptable as a minimum. He suggested the same minimum ought to be imposed for girls as for boys, if a minimum really had to be imposed. They were not to be put off.

Challenged to a hat, I helped myself to one of Emily's more outrageous items – a vintage American velvet drum with a halfveil – so they sent me home, hat or no hat. It didn't help that I arrived at quarter to twelve having spent all morning getting naked and stoned while fetching the outrageous hat.

So my second phase of home schooling began. Except that I was hardly ever at home. And there was absolutely no schooling involved. Edward spent a lot of time trying to negotiate with the school over my taking exams there as an external candidate, but I hadn't done any of the coursework so they refused. They said I would disturb the other candidates. I guess I had been disturbing the other candidates for about four years at this point. Disturbing the other candidates was my special skill.

Without an exam to sit, there didn't seem to be any point being home for the maths tutor Edward organised. Or much point in coming home the night before to be ready in the morning. So I spent most of the day pretending to be a college student, wearing Emily's identity badge from the year before if I happened to be on campus. I found the college library was a good place to hide, and built a wall around me made of the largest books I could find.

Art books were the best. They were huge, heavy, and I could turn over the pages and have something to look at without bothering much with the text. Also, in the art section of the library my shaved head and strange collection of clothes did not attract attention. There were plenty of other shaved heads and odd home-made garments around. When I eventually went to the college to do my art diploma, all the librarians already knew me. And it turned out I had accidentally absorbed quite a bit of information from the books I was using as a shield.

I watched the other students going to the college canteen and buying cheesy chips or all-day breakfasts and felt superior to them. If I got hungry I stole sweets from supermarkets, and when I did go home I always said I had already eaten. At Emily's flat there was food in the fridge. Odd things I had never tried before. Olives and feta in little tubs. Different kinds of nuts. I didn't question how they got there. As long as it didn't look like a meal I would eat it. I made a secret rule never to use a knife and fork.

At the end of the day the sandwich shop sold pasties for 50p and I would sometimes eat one of these out of the bag, not looking at what I ate. If I didn't look at it, it didn't count. At home I ate apples by cutting them up into tiny slices and smuggling them into my mouth. If I ate enough of them I threw up, so they didn't count either. Emily always asked me if Edward had given me anything to eat, and if I had accepted it. She was pleased with me if I said no.

At first she liked me being there all the time. She didn't have to wait for me to come off the school bus and take off my uniform. I could be there all afternoon with the heat turned up, wearing nothing at all, smoking her cigarettes and eating her olives. But then she got bored. She started saying, 'When is your dad going to come and take you home? Doesn't he care where you are? Does he even know?'

She started asking lots of questions about Edward. And about my mother. She wanted me to go away, but she didn't want me to go back to him. I understood in some way that she saw him as the enemy, and even though she didn't want to keep me for herself, she still didn't want me to go back to him.

I could see Edward didn't like the relationship, but I didn't know why. He asked me odd questions, about her mother, about her flat. Emily told me he was probably homophobic. I said he didn't ask me why I was seeing a girl. He asked all kinds of other things. Things about her mother. She laughed at that. She said, why is he suddenly interested in how I feel? After everything he has done. What had he done?

Quite often when I arrived at Emily's flat now the place would be empty. I would let myself in and try reading some of the doorstop books, or take a pot of nuts out of the fridge and suck the salt off them, then spit them out again. I cut olives into four and ate them a quarter at a time.

Sometimes the door would be bolted and she would have someone else there. A boy. He looked too ordinary for me to consider him a serious rival. He wore T-shirts with collars on them. He had tiny pimples all over his cheeks. And he was impossibly tall. He was a giant next to her. How could she stand it? Surely he would crush her, or smother her by accident. How could she possibly have sex with someone like that?

I sat on the landing outside her door listening to the noises. Then I listened for them to stop. Then I waited until I heard him put his clothes on. I could hear the clunk of his belt buckle against the floor, the stamp of his feet back into his shoes. Then I would knock on the door. She didn't bother to let me in herself. She would make the boy do that.

To prove I didn't care I would make myself a cup of black tea. The boy would say, 'What is her problem? Why is she so weird?' And Emily looked proud of me then.

'Her mother disappeared in mysterious circumstances. She doesn't like to go home.'

Mysterious circumstances. That was a new set of words for it. It made me sound like a character in a detective story. Not a reject. Not a shivering flaky-skinned little weirdo with hardly any hair and scabby half-done piercings around the edge of her ears. I was a mystery.

When the boy was there Emily enjoyed saying outrageous things about me, about my mother, about Edward. She liked to shock the boy. I was one of her collection of interesting objects.

'Her mother just disappeared. No trace of her. And her father left the place like a museum. Untouched. No one else is allowed to move in. He won't let anyone touch it.' That wasn't exactly what I had told her, but I didn't argue. I was enjoying being the Mystery Girl, the centre of an Unsolved Crime.

12

Gothic

The man in the moon
Came down too soon
And asked his way to Norwich

He went by the south
And burned his mouth
By eating cold pease porridge

The only thing Emily still liked about me was my mysterious circumstance. The only stories she wanted to hear were the ones where Edward was some kind of gothic villain. The only way I could get her to send the boy away was if I promised to tell her about our deserted house. The ghosts in the stairwell. The angels in the windows. The stories of drowned girls my mother told me. The one who lay murdered in the dark pool, where the water would never run clear after that night, no matter what they did to it. And the other story, the one with the hat.

In this story, the girl left her hat pinned to the bank of the pit where she went in to drown herself. She was pregnant, and when she told her young man about the baby he said he had already promised to marry another girl in the village and she was pregnant too. One of the men going to work in the field saw the hat, but he didn't say anything until later in the day, and when a group of them went back to look she was already dead. And her baby too.

Because that was the kind of thing she wanted to hear, I told her about the strange sounds the house made when the rain was running down the lane and bubbling back out of the drains, I told her about the badgers digging holes in the orchard, the grunting bear-like snufflings and crunchings, the trails of red sandstone they left where they had cleaned out their homes. I told her about the bats who lived in the old barn, the whiskery flicks of them circling the yard around the back door.

Why had we left? she asked. Was the place haunted? I said my mother thought so. It was one of the things she liked about the place. And did I see ghosts there? I didn't want to disappoint her. I turned my face from her when I made up my more outrageous stories.

While I lay on my stomach and invented ghosts and demons and evil spirits rising from the cellar – there was never a cellar – Emily ran her fingers over my shoulder blades and kissed the small of my back. She said she had read that the nerve endings on the back were so far apart I wouldn't know if she touched me with one, two or three fingers. I didn't care how many fingers she was pressing into my back. I only wanted to keep them there.

Her favourite story was the one I made up about a small boy ghost who appeared at the bottom of the stairs, so clear and complete that anyone staying in the house would ask, who was the little boy in the nightshirt, the one at the bottom of the stairs? I claimed no dog would ever walk down the hallway after dark.

I said the ghosts did not like certain pictures, and that after you hung the pictures the ghosts would come in the night and take them down. You would hear them crash to the floor, and you'd know they didn't like them.

I told her there was a patch of cold air by the cellar door you shivered to walk through, no matter how warm it was in the house. I think I heard these stories from Lindsey, and they were almost certainly about the village pub. But once I started telling them, they began to attach themselves to our old house in my mind. After a while I couldn't remember where they belonged. I couldn't even remember if my parents had ever described our old house as haunted.

Emily wanted to know all kinds of things about our old house, and about my mother's disappearance. What date, exactly, had she gone missing? What had we left behind in the house, and what had we brought with us?

The decisions about what to bring and what to leave had happened piecemeal, boxes of toys and kitchen implements packed up and then forgotten, bags of bedding and towels left in the wrong cupboard or gone mouldy when we stacked them in the back porch. Mismatched wellies and walking boots in piles by the doors of both houses – no one ever seemed to have a complete pair when they needed one.

At first the idea had been to leave the Old House furnished, to make it more saleable, but then the things we left behind took on a desolate, collapsed look, and we were supposed to clear them out, but we didn't finish the job properly. The books Edward needed for work all came with him, but others were left behind. Novels, gardening books, picture books Joe had scribbled on or torn, old maps, the remains of Great-Uncle Matthew's *National Geographic* collection stuck together and fading under the window seats.

Edward asked a firm of house clearers and when they said £200 he thought that was what they were offering for the remaining books, but it was what they wanted him to pay them to take it all away. He said no thanks, he'd do it himself. But there were always so many other things to do at the weekend: school laundry and shopping and Joe's baby gym club and homework and marking and play dates and hoovering.

If we set off for the old house with a picnic and a box of firelighters and a supply of determination we were always undone before midday among piles of baby clothes or sprouting tulip bulbs or nests of mice in our old blankets. We brought back half-hearted boxes of things to sort, and left them piled up in the porch until we got fed up with tripping over them, and threw them into the bin without looking inside.

If the house was still full of things, Emily asked, what could be hidden there? How could we be sure we had searched every inch of it? Why had Edward left certain things behind, why didn't he want them any more? When I told her I had been banned from going there myself, after the last time I ran away from school, her ears pricked up again. Didn't I have a right to go there? Wasn't it my home as well as his? What was he trying to keep from me? Why had I not tried to go back? Couldn't I see it was all suspicious? Not really.

And now I wasn't even going to school, why couldn't we all go back and live there? It was hard to explain. The truth was, the house was still officially for sale, but there were more and more things wrong with it and there was never enough money to mend it now we had to pay for the New House as well. The barn was listed so we weren't allowed to change anything in it, but the beams were unsafe.

We could sell the barn, maybe, if someone wanted to turn it into a house, but then we would have to sell the drive for them to get to it. Someone asked to rent the house, but then they found out the heating was broken and the back door didn't shut properly and if we borrowed enough to mend it we would have to sell it anyway, so it stood empty. But none of that felt possible to say. Or possible for me to say. So instead I talked about the creaks in the stairwell and the cries of the vixen in the garden that could pierce the soul.

Emily narrowed her eyes and pushed her glasses up her nose to signal she had something important to say. She said, 'I think he has his own reasons. Reasons for holding on to it.' She said she had met someone who talked to the dead. A medium. A person who painted auras for a living. This person could look at the air around you, and paint the spirits and colours of your dreams and your past. She said she was sure that if we went to the house the aura painter would find out the secret. I said, 'I don't think Edward would allow that.' Her eyes flashed fury.

'Isn't it your mystery as well as his? Don't you have a right to know?' I didn't have an answer to that one.

So right then and there Emily started packing what we needed for the journey: a pack of cards, the remains of a half-bottle of whisky stolen from someone's pocket in the nightclub cloakroom, cigarette papers, weed, a credit card, a lighter, a candle and a piece of painted card that the aura painter had given her with a kind of incantation on the back in red felt-tip. I didn't try to stop her. I thought if we set off on a journey there was no way the boy could follow us. It was ages since we had done anything without him being there.

I should have warned her there is almost no public transport to our village. After the train arrived in Whitchurch we had missed the last bus of the day to the village, so we had to get the one that goes along the main road and ask the driver to stop in the layby nearest to the top of the lane. It's at least a mile from there to the centre of the village, all of it in total darkness. About halfway down that road the mobile signal stopped. It didn't make much difference because we were using it as a torch, so it ran out of battery.

As soon as the torch went out Emily started wandering all over the road, clutching onto me or standing still and shrieking at me to come back, where had I gone? I was right there next to her. I didn't understand the problem. As long as you keep one foot on the metalled road you can feel and hear the edge of it. And when the hedge is lower you can see enough by moonlight to follow the slight reflection on the surface. Even in the darkest stretches you can feel the slight camber and keep to the centre of it. It had never occurred to me until I was walking down Duckington Lane in the dark with Emily that walking steadily along an unlit road after dark is a life skill. I had taken it for granted.

For the first time in our relationship I had an advantage. We were on my territory now, where I knew the frightening stories and which of them I had made up, and I knew how to stop and stand totally still on the road right next to her without warning so she would have no idea where I had gone.

For most of the way I took pity on her, held her hand, spoke to her in an even, kindly tone. But by the old dump I couldn't resist telling her that was where the girl had drowned, the one with the hat pinned to the bank, though in fact I have no idea which pit that might have been. She crept closer to me, her sharp little hands digging into my arm, scratching me through the loops of my unravelling jumper.

There's one street lamp in the village, by the old telephone box, but it doesn't work. The lights were all on in the pub though, and the sight of the glowing windows cheered Emily up so much she practically broke into a run. But as soon as we pushed open the heavy door and stepped inside I knew we had made a mistake.

Emily didn't realise there are rules about who goes on which side of the bar, where the men stand, where the women go. She walked right up to the men's side, and asked if anyone could lend her a charger. I watched the men stand aside for her, glance down at her muddy feet in pointed velvet shoes and turn away without replying.

Emily didn't seem to understand what that meant. She was as lost in here as she was walking down an unlit lane. She asked again, more loudly, and waved her unresponsive phone in the air to demonstrate. The group of men edged away from her, nodded to each other and shuffled away to stand around the dartboard, leaving her alone at the bar.

She climbed up on a bar stool to lean over the bar to call someone over to help her. The young woman behind the bar was someone I recognised from primary school, one of three sisters who were all very athletic, though I wasn't sure which she was. I thought it was probably the middle one, Stephanie. They were all about six feet tall with long blonde hair. Her eyes flicked from me to Emily and back to me, where she gave me a barely perceptible nod, to let me know she knew who I was.

I stood on the correct side of the bar, the women's side, and beckoned Emily over. She just stared at me and said very loudly, 'Come over here, you idiot, there's loads of seats free.' I couldn't very well explain the seats at the bar were free because the men they belonged to were avoiding standing next to her, and were waiting for someone to tell her to leave. She was still waving her phone around and shouting for service, so I went round to where she was sitting, and asked her to come back to the other side of the bar with me.

'Why? What's wrong with these seats? It's like in that film, you know, *American Werewolf in London*, where they go into the village pub and it's called the Dead Sheep or something. No, the Slaughtered Sheep.' Probably-Stephanie was standing right next to us.

'You mean the Slaughtered Lamb,' she said, and stood with her hands on her hips. She held out her hand to take the phone and plugged it in behind the bar.

Emily said, 'I'll have a double vodka and orange juice. And

two packets of salted nuts.' Probably-Stephanie put two packets of nuts on the bar.

'£1.60. I know that one, and she's sixteen maybe. And you look about the same.'

Emily narrowed her eyes and considered making her usual fuss about being nearly NINETEEN as a matter of fact, and discrimination against size was a REAL THING in case you didn't know, then decided against it, and handed over the money for the peanuts. She had to jump down from the bar stool, she was so small, and as she did Probably-Stephanie looked down at me, and shook her head again. We didn't really mind about the vodka, as we still had the remains of the half-bottle of whisky in the rucksack, and we took turns taking little swigs out of it behind our jumpers. We thought we were being secretive about it but Probably-Stephanie went to fetch the manager from the other bar to glare at us, so we weren't as secret as we thought. In a village you are always the daughter of someone. Never just yourself. That's difficult if your mother is famous for walking out, and you come from a house that is falling down. I saw the men around the dartboard looking over at me, conferring, checking I was the one, who, you know, they had that bad business over by the Cape. The Cape is what people call the turn in the road before you get to our gate.

I split each peanut carefully in half, sucked the salt off, then spat it out and lined it up with the others along the table. Emily didn't know about villages. In minutes everyone would know I had been there, with my hair cut off, with a strange-looking girl with rainbow hair on half her head and a lot of piercings. The smell of weed on our clothes would already be under discussion.

They were probably already saying how we were always a weird lot, they're the ones who, you know, they had the Richards girls to look after them, after, you know. The little lad would be, what? Seven now? They moved away. Can't blame them. After what went on. Looks like that girl went wrong. State of her hair.

From the pub it is another half-mile to the house, all of it unlit. The road turns on right angles around the edge of fields. There's a huge barn along one side of the road just before our lane. It blocks any light from the sky. I've always welcomed it. There are warm sounds and smells of the cattle on the other side of the wall. The smell of wet hay and silage and cow's breath means I am only one field away from the end of our drive. The road is usually a bit green and slippery at this point too, but I had never thought of it as unpleasant.

Now we were nearly there I was excited to show Emily our house. In the morning she would see the walled garden and the orchard and the cobbled yard. Even in the dark she might admire the gentle sounds of it, the beautiful windows and wooden shutters, the smell of old wood and something like cinnamon, the smell of home. I would light a fire. It would be romantic. She didn't say so, but surely she loved me? How could she not love my home?

She clutched at my arm so hard her fingernails were digging deep into the sides of my elbows. She had stopped shouting at everything, and instead kept up an almost constant stream of whimpering complaints. Emily's expensive velvet feet skidded across the green slime and she screamed out, 'What is that disgusting smell?'

'It's the cows, stupid! That's what cows smell like?'

'Why are they so disgusting? There's something on my feet!' I pulled further away from her. I felt offended on behalf of the cows. And the lane. And my home. But I couldn't leave her there alone in the dark. I had to put my hand out to her, and lead her along the wall past the farm gate and around the turn in the hedge to the start of our lane.

'We're here. You can stop shouting now.'

'Where? Where are we? I can't see anything! That stuff is still on my feet!'

'Well, it's always slippery this time of year. When the cows are inside.'

'I don't care! Just take me home right now. I can't stand another second of this stink and this shit and this, this SHIT!'

'But we're nearly there. We'll never get a bus till the morning. It's alright.'

'I'm not going to your stupid haunted house.'

'It's not haunted. Not really. Just cold.'

Emily was crying now. 'But you said, you said ...'

I steered her by the shoulders round the corner of the hedge and into our lane. The lane is narrow, with high hedges, and deep rutted sides, and even on a moonlit night there are parts of it where no light falls. No one had been looking after it for a while, and some of the hedges had fallen in under their own weight, nearly filling the path, and in other places the brambles had sent out long strands that tangled into our hair and our faces, and there was no way of seeing them before they caught us.

The ground was worse here, too, with deeper mud. The gravel had washed away, and the grass had grown back down the middle of the path. I don't know what it was about the lane or the light falling on the mud or the hard going under foot that reminded me of the time of year. Something about the moonlight falling through a gap in the hedge. Or the cold. Or the smell of the lane in winter, its particular, cold-mud smell. Something that stopped me in my tracks, turned my empty stomach to ice. I pulled away from her.

'Emily! What's the date today?' She didn't move. 'What's the date? It's February now, right? But what day?'

She pulled her bony arms away from me and tucked them around her tiny body, and I realised in a rush the depths of her enmity, the real danger she posed. How had I underestimated her until now? She had brought me here tonight, on this anniversary, knowing Edward would have to come and find me. I had lost count of the days since I stopped going to school. I had lost all track of time. But Emily hadn't.

13

Talking to the Dead

Have you got a sister?
The beggarman kissed her.

Have you got a brother?
He's made of India rubber.

Have you got a baby?
He's made of bread and gravy.

I was frightened now. Frightened of how upset Edward would be. Frightened of what we had started. I considered going back to the pub and calling home, but it would be shut by the time I got there. And what would I do with Emily? I could hardly leave her in the middle of the lane. Her phone had already switched off again. The nearest place was home. My feet were cold and wet, so I carried on down the drive, holding on to Emily to stop her from screaming or falling into the hedge. I pushed open the gate to the backyard, dragged her across the slippery cobbles, shouldered open the rain-swollen back door, and breathed in the smell of home: cinnamon, bread, lambswool, clean sand.

I tried the light switch. Nothing. No surprise. I didn't think Edward would be paying for electricity in an empty house. But that meant I couldn't get Emily to charge her phone. And that meant no way of calling home and getting away before morning. I lit the candle we'd brought with us, and used it to look under the sink for a jam jar and the basket of nightlights and saucers we kept in there. I put Emily's candle into a jar by dripping wax into the bottom and setting it inside.

'How did you know to do that?' she said. I shrugged. Didn't everyone know how to do that? What did they do when the electricity went off?

Now we had a light I led her into the living room, but she was still whimpering and clutching my sleeves, jumping at every scuff of our feet, shouting things like 'Is that a mouse?' and 'Where's the door to the cellar?' and 'Why is it so cold in here?' At least I had an easy answer to that one.

'Because there's no heating. We'll light a fire.'

'How? How do you light a fire?'

'How can you not know how to light a fire?'

She stared at me, her eyes huge behind her glasses, the candlelight flickering across the lenses like a cheap special effect. I had no sympathy for her. She had brought me here as bait. I had no idea why she wanted to punish Edward, but I saw our whole relationship now as a trick, an elaborate trap. She had never wanted me for myself. She wanted me as a way to torture my father. It made no sense to me, but now she had got me here I wasn't going to make her night in a haunted house any easier.

I set the candle on the hearth where I could see if there was any kindling to start a fire. If I built a good enough fire it would light the room as well. We had left the wooden shutters closed, so the room was even darker than the night outside. There were only a few decent logs for the fire but the unravelling wicker basket they were in would make good kindling if I could find some paper dry enough to start it. On the shelves next to the fire there were a few rejected picture books too scribbled on for us to bother packing, the remains of a jigsaw in a broken cardboard box, some wooden building blocks with the paper pictures peeling off them. I tore the pages out of *Bear's Adventure* and twisted them into firelighters.

Emily stayed right next to me, hovering around me and twitching. I handed her some pages to twist, but she just placed them flat into the grate. I redid all her pages, and lit the wicker basket kindling, using the light from this to search for anything else we could burn. A few cracked wooden spoons. Some children's paintbrushes. A cutlery tray. A stack of empty picture frames.

As the fire gathered pace, Emily moved further away from the hearth to look for something to sit on. She gathered some heavy dust sheets and a disgusting knitted blanket we used to use for visiting dogs, and built them into a kind of nest by the fire. I left her there and went upstairs to look for more bedding.

It felt wet, but it was mostly just the cold of it. I found a sleeping bag, a few blankets. It would have to do. Emily piled them all around her. She looked very small and very young sitting in the middle of her nest with her knees up around her ears, staring wide-eyed at the corners of the room as if she expected something to jump out at her. As I headed upstairs again to see what else I could find, I couldn't resist saying, 'I hope you're not afraid of mice?' I hung about a bit on the landing just for the fun of it. It wasn't often I had the upper hand.

When I came down again Emily had set out her playing cards in a circle in front of the fire, more or less marking the outer limits of where you could feel the heat. She put the candle in its jar carefully in the middle, and started to read the words off her little piece of card. I don't know what she was expecting. Something dramatic. My stomach rumbled. Emily looked disgusted.

'Can you find another jar, or a glass? You're supposed to put your fingers on top of a glass.'

'You're supposed to share the fucking whisky with the use of a glass as well.' I stomped off to the kitchen with the candle to look again under the sink and turned up a Thomas the Tank Engine plastic beaker and a peanut-butter jar with a dead spider in the bottom. I shared out the rest of the whisky between the glasses, pouring it far enough from the candle that she couldn't see she was drinking the dead spider. When I'd emptied the Thomas the Tank Engine beaker I turned it upside down in the middle of the circle as a kind of dare. I didn't expect anything to happen. Other than Emily scaring herself silly every time a branch blew against the back door. And there were a lot of branches around the back door.

Emily rolled a joint on the floor, and the first one came up too damp, so she started again, on her rucksack. I held out my hand for my turn, but she stared past me, smoking determinedly, puffing out each breath in a kind of aggressive rhythm. I took my wet socks off and draped them across one of the broken picture frames in the hearth to dry. I enjoyed stretching them out, wringing them, I enjoyed her horror, the way she huddled her own feet even closer under the blanket in response.

When she had finished her joint, she propped the piece of painted card against her rucksack where she could see the felttip words, put her fingers back on the Thomas the Tank Engine beaker, and closed her eyes. I don't know what was written on that card, if it was supposed to be in any real language, or if it was just some made-up stuff someone decided she was stupid enough to buy from them, but some of it sounded like my name. I suppose it might have been a variant on 'Om'. But in any case I didn't like it.

I picked up her peanut-butter jar of whisky, spider or no spider, to drink it myself as payback for the unshared joint, and I swear I didn't squeeze it tight or try to break it, but it splintered dramatically in my hand, pieces flying far away from the lit area by the fire out into the darkness of the room, and I noticed my hand was wet, and stinging, and I thought, that's blood, and then there was a crashing sound upstairs.

Whenever I tell anyone about this, they say, well, probably you broke the glass because you were angry, or you heard the crash and that startled you, so you broke the glass, or the glass was already broken but you didn't notice in the dark. All I can say is, that's not how I remember it. I remember the chanting, glass flying out in all directions, the blood and whisky together in my palm, then the crash, then Emily's scream.

Somehow among all that the candle went out. I probably knocked it over when I jumped up. I ran towards the stairs and the noise, and then ran back to relight the candle, and I realised my bare feet were wet as well as my hand. More blood. Whatever it was making the noise upstairs was still up there, knocking things over or bumping into things. I didn't think for a second it was a ghost. It sounded too heavy and real and erratic. But it was in my house, and I did want to know what it was.

On the landing was a huge black bird. It must have been a crow. It was dragging one of its wings along behind it, and half taking off, and landing badly, and throwing itself lopsidedly against the tall window at the end of the landing. The crashing sound was the door to the end bedroom that was banging in its frame in the cold draught blasting through it.

The bird must have been in the bedroom. Perhaps our opening the door downstairs had blown the door open, but now the bird was on the landing, and the door to the bedroom banging in its frame was scaring it silly and it couldn't find its way out. Maybe it had been trapped, starving, in the bedroom for days, and we had disturbed it.

I ran past it to the end window, and pulled up the lower pane on its sash. I knew there was a trick to this window, because for some reason I was not allowed to open it or close it myself. Something to do with a stick. But this was no time for trying to find a stick on the floor in the dark, so I shoved the window up as high as I could, and stepped away. It crashed back down unevenly in the frame, splintering. That was it. You had to prop the window on a stick. One of the sashes was broken. Too late. And how would the bird get out now?

It was my parents' bedroom door banging to and fro, and now that the wind was coming in from the landing window as well, it was louder than ever. I ran back behind the bird, chasing it up and down the landing, trying to get it to go back into the bedroom. It was not keen, and, to be honest, nor was I. I never liked going into that room after my mother left. No one did. Edward had moved into Joe's room right away, to look after him at night, he said, but neither of them ever moved back.

Someone must have gone in and emptied her cupboards and drawers and taken her books from beside the bed and washed the bedding and folded it into the airing cupboard, but it wasn't us. It was probably Mrs Wynne. I never saw it happen. It must have been done when I was at school. I remember seeing it stripped, empty, the blind pulled down, patches on the walls where the pictures used to be, the mattress covered with a plain blanket, but I couldn't tell you when I saw that. Perhaps years later.

But now I had to go in and close the door behind me and prop open the window and gently, patiently, shoo the bird towards its limping, half-flight out into the pear tree outside. I was aware I was leaving bloody footprints behind me, and smudges of blood from my hand on the window and the door and the walls. When the sad bird had half jumped, half flown out of the window I fastened the shutters, plunging myself into total darkness to find my way back along the walls by bloody fingertips, through the trails of blood and feathers and soot and dust to the door.

Emily was waiting on the landing, sitting hunched over her candle in the jar, shivering under the best blanket I'd found.

'Is it gone?'

'Yeah.'

'It's freezing now you've broken that big window.'

'It's the sash. It's snapped. You're supposed to prop it on a stick. I forgot.'

'What are you talking about? What the fuck is a sash? You are such a weirdo! What is that all over your feet?'

'Blood. From the broken glass.'

'I told you they were here.'

'They?'

'Was this the room where he died?'

He? What was she talking about?

'My Great-Uncle Matthew? The one who gave the house to my dad? He died in the nursing home.'

'Not him, no. Your brother. The one who died.'

What was she talking about? My brother was alive and well and living in the West Midlands.

'I mean, losing one relative is bad enough. But two in one place? You really think it's coincidence?'

I stared at her. In the candlelight her face looked carved, waxy, unhealthy.

'Do you think that was her?'

'What?'

'Your mother? I used the chant to summon your mother. I asked her to tell me where he had hidden her. Then the bird flew in. Do you think she's in the bedroom?'

'It was a bird. They get stuck. It might have been there for days, looking for a way out.'

'It might have been your brother.'

'Unlikely. Seeing as he's in his bed near Wolverhampton.

And last time I looked he was a skinny little blond boy, not a ruddy great crow.'

'Not that brother. The dead brother. I summoned him as well.'

'Well stop fucking summoning things, will you? Especially things that break our windows and shit on our floors. Or try summoning something useful. Like a pizza delivery or something. Hot chocolate. And stop talking shit about a dead brother as well. It's not funny. Just leave Joe out of it.'

'I keep telling you. Not Joe. The other one.'

'I haven't got another one.'

'Not now he's dead you don't.'

'What the fuck are you talking about?' I started down the stairs, my wet hand slippery on the banister, prickles of glass sharp under my feet. But I felt no pain. I was burning in indignation and anger, but under it, hotter still, was fear. I recognised it and rejected in the same instant. And that, too, was familiar: the knowing and the refusing to know overlapping each other in the split second, the effort it took like a double breath, a trip-step stumble of the heart.

Downstairs, Emily occupied the warm spot in her nest by the fire, while I paced the perimeter, grinding glass into the soles of my feet, looking for more and more ridiculous things to burn on the fire. I couldn't stop shaking. I picked up one of the abandoned dining chairs with a sunken seat, and started smashing it down onto the edge of the stone hearth as hard as I could. Emily scrunched herself more tightly into her blankets and wrapped her arms around her head.

When the legs of the chair were loose, I jammed them roughly into the fireplace even though half of them stuck out over the hearth rug. The fire flared up for a few minutes around the woven seat of the chair, then died down again. I drank the last of the whisky from the bottle.

'Alright then,' I said, 'but quickly, before I die of cold or hunger. What are you talking about?'

And she told me. The story my parents had kept from me. How the year they came to this house they had a baby boy, born in the big bedroom at the end of the landing. And he never breathed. He was buried at the old chapel on the river path, the one no one used any more. And then they had me. That was the whole story. Her mother had told her. How Edward had married someone who had been his student and taken her to live in an old house in the country, and then their baby had died.

My first instinct was to deny it. Shout, 'Liar!'

I did shout. For quite a while. I couldn't think of a better word than liar for a while, so I kept on with that even as I felt my world resettle around me in a new and more horrible version.

I hated her then. For knowing. For being the one to tell me. Because even as I was shouting, 'Liar! I hate you! Liar!' I was remembering my mother singing me that special song, 'Green gravel, green gravel, your grass is so green.' And I knew now who she was singing it for. A burial song for a new baby, washed in new milk and wrapped in silk, his name a secret no one would ever say out loud again, written down in gold ink and buried with him in the Green Chapel where we used to go and light a candle. Every winter. Sometime after Christmas.

I remembered singing the special song all along the river:

I'll wash you in new milk
and wrap you in silk,
And write down your name
in a gold pen and ink.

The song was conclusive. I had known all my life that when I met my mother again, and neither of us was recognisable, this was the song I had to sing to tell her it was me. This was the song that had to be sung on a particular day at the Green Chapel to appease the dead.

At the Green Chapel. Near the bridge that floods in winter. Where she went into the water. Where they found her footprint. Distinct, because she had left without her wellies or good shoes, and whatever she had on her feet when she set off must have got lost on the way, and the prints were there, with the toes marked out in the mud, or they were there the first time they looked and took photos, but when they went back the cows had been down to the river and mashed up all the mud banks with their hooves and nothing was left.

And when they came to check the first photos they were not very clear, after all, and someone had done something wrong in logging them as evidence, because they assumed the right people would go back the next day with the right cameras and do it properly. Her footprints in the mud became inadmissible. So officially there is no record of where she might have gone into the water or what she might have had on her feet.

But now I was shouting, 'Liar! Liar! I hate you!' and Emily was shrinking back into the nest of blankets and her shoulders were raised against the attack like pointed wings, and with every shout I knew more certainly that she was right and I was wrong. And I knew there was some reason her mother knew about it, something to do with Edward.

I caught the whiff of something I recognised, something that stops you seeing what's there in front of your face: shame. I recognised the shameful anger of knowing you are deeply, irreversibly wrong. So I carried on shouting and breaking things for as long as I could because I knew when the quiet started after that I would be in a worse world than the one where I lived before.

Perhaps I would have gone on shouting all night, but I had underestimated the village. The communal memory of the village. The conversation around the bar after we left. The date on the wall. The way the talk went round and round and ended with the bar manager calling Lindsey's mum and dad. Everyone knows their number, because they run the local taxi, and they knew Edward's number, and Edward called Emily's parents, who called the police.

But the police have other things to do than chase off to deserted houses to see if a pair of teenagers in unlikely clothes are smoking dope or doing anything else they shouldn't, and Emily's parents lived closer to the motorway and didn't have to wake up a seven-year-old and put him in a sleeping bag in his car seat, and they had a really big four-wheel drive that made it up the lane no trouble, so they got there a full forty minutes before anyone else.

Emily recognised the sound of her own family car, and was out of her nest and through the back door by the time the lights swung into the last stretch of the lane, running out of the haunted house away from the bleeding, screaming witch and the black-winged ghosts, into the arms of her mother. There was never any discussion about blame. It was my house. I had brought her there. And anyone could see I was raving drunk, screaming abuse and pouring blood out of every extremity.

I think I threw random things as well as abuse at Emily as she ran out of the building. One of the things was a half-burnt chair leg that lay smouldering on the cobbles while Emily's mother gathered her poor daughter into the warm coat she had ready, and tucked her into the back of their Range Rover with the heat turned up.

Then she turned on me. I remember that, as a precursor to her annihilation of my character and behaviour, she unpinned her hair from the comb on the back of her head, shook it loose, then tied it back up again. I tried to back away from her, and slam the door, but it was swollen with damp and sprang open again, so the entire character assassination was punctuated with door slammings and openings and screams from me, and, towards the end, a low mumble of something else that I understood to be her husband joining in more quietly.

I wasn't listening to anything she said. But there was a lot of it. The sheer quantity was impressive. I understood by how long it went on that I was a very bad person indeed. Even worse than they already knew. And that was bad enough.

For some reason I had an empty whisky bottle in one hand, and at some pause in their list of my evil doings, I threw it into the yard, where it shattered on the cobbles, but it barely interrupted the flow of her invective. I was impressed.

I think she ended on something like, 'You can explain yourself to the police when they get here.' Which made me laugh out loud. I had been explaining my unworthiness to the police on a regular basis for about eight years at this point. But now she had finally finished I shouted, 'And you can explain to me why Edward told you about his dead baby, when no one else in the world knows about it, not even me and Joe. And why you thought it was a good idea to tell your stupid daughter to tell me.' There was a long pause. The headlights were facing down the lane, so I could not see the two faces of her mother and father. And Emily's father said, 'What baby?' So I knew it was something between Edward and Emily's mother. Something her husband didn't know about. Then their shadows stepped further from the light, and I heard the car doors slam shut.

I thought they were going to leave me there alone all night. I didn't know that Edward was coming too until I saw his car arrive behind theirs, blocking them in. He left the engine running because Joe only stays asleep in cars as long as the engine is running. Then he picked his way around their car, getting tangled up in stray bits of hedge, and crunched his way over the broken bottle in the yard to the doorway. He hugged me so hard he lifted me off the ground, and that might have been the first time he realised how thin I had been getting. He was crying, and by now I was too. We both said sorry a lot at the same time.

'I'm sorry. I didn't know the date till we got here.'

'It's not you. This is nothing to do with you. It's my fault.'

'She told me about the baby that died. She told me when we got here.'

'Jonathan? She told you about Jonathan?'

'Is that his name?'

'Jonathan. Yes. But nobody knows. I mean, it was never, how did she?'

'You never told me.'

'Your mother wanted to tell you when you were older. It never felt right. It was never the right time.'

'But everyone knows!'

'No. No, that's not right. It was never. I mean, hang on, have you got anything on your feet? Only there's something nasty on the cobbles here.' He carried me to the gate, then had to put me down. There's no room to carry someone around a parked car on that lane, especially one as big as theirs.

So I edged my way along the grass at the side, adding mud to my cuts, smearing bloody handprints over their windows along the way, and climbed into the back seat next to Joe, sleeping open-mouthed in his car seat, and the air damp with snores and the heating vents on full and the smell of toast crusts and orange-juice boxes. I unwrapped one side of his blanket and put it over my bare feet and lay curled up tight in the one empty seat.

I could hear the music of their argument, but none of the words. Three adult voices and occasional car doors. The whisky and starvation made my head spin. I closed my eyes tight and held on to the edge of the seat as if that would keep out the noise.

And then the police turned up. Their headlights filled the back seat as they pulled up and parked behind us, three cars jammed one behind the other, all pointing at our old house with a long way to reverse up a muddy track to get out.

The police wanted to know if I was okay. I said yes, but they saw the blood on my hands and feet when they opened the car door, and got out their first-aid kit. They couldn't help noticing while they were wrapping my feet and hands in dressings that my skin was cut and scarred and dry and flaky and yellow, and that my bones were sticking out. They asked about my drug use, and my cutting, and my eating, and told Edward to take me to the GP in the morning.

Once the police knew we were both safe, they reversed all the way back to the road, then we did, then Emily's parents. Between us we churned up a lot of mud and gravel and destroyed the grass verges. We stalled twice and Joe woke up, so I was distracted trying to soothe him back to sleep as we reversed into the road and turned away from the house for the last time.

And even if I had looked behind me at the roof line and the row of chimneys in the moonlight, it was probably too early to see that the tamped-down remains of our fire had made its way somehow into the crow's nest in the chimney, and the fire would be fed all night by the air through the broken windows and half-open doors and would spread from the chimney to the roof beams until the whole of the upper floor was full of slow, purposeful, unstoppable smoke, and that it would gradually work its way through every room, sucking the life out of the old house from the inside, until the whole place collapsed on itself.

There's no way we could have peered far enough ahead in the darkness as we drove away to foresee how this collapse of our home would mean we would never have the money to return to it now, and how the people who bought it at auction that year would remake it so completely that we would never recognise it again. I did ask about going back to see it and say goodbye, but Edward said it would be too sad for me, and besides, I was not exactly well enough to go anywhere or do anything for quite a long time after that. Our world shrank into the shape of the New House, and I shrank under the covers in my wrong-smelling room, drew the curtains on the wrong view outside the window, and tried to relearn how to eat and sleep and be well. Of all the things I had to relearn after my mother left, these were perhaps the hardest ones.

Because that's the other thing I remember about that night: hunger. As a background to gaining and losing a brother in a matter of seconds, there was a constant rumbling of hunger. As soon as we entered the house I felt it. I can pinpoint the moment. Not in the pub, sucking the salt off peanut halves and spitting them out into my hand. Not on the walk there.

It was the moment when I pushed the door open. I was looking for a jar for the candle, and things to burn, and all the time I was rummaging through oddments on kitchen shelves I was wondering what there might be in the house to eat. A tin of tuna, perhaps. I was hoping for a tin of tuna.

And while I was watching Emily set out her circle of cards and chanting the words on her piece of old cardboard, my stomach was churning and rumbling and bubbling away, longing for food. The more I breathed in the smell of the floorboards and the sandy smell of the stone floors, the catch of flame on the first pieces of kindling, the crunch of the wooden jigsaw blocks peeling their ancient paper coverings into the fireplace, the more my stomach called out for food.

Not just daring-myself-to-steal-a-packet-of-Smarties hungry. Nothing that a pot of olives would cure. I wanted a jacket potato with butter and cheese. I wanted brown toast and Marmite. I wanted a roast chicken dinner with gravy.

It's not that easy, starting to eat again. Your dead mother

doesn't meet you in your old house in the form of a crow and blow into your nostrils so they suddenly smell food and want to eat, and that is it. It takes a long time to put right, and it is much more to do with meal plans and meetings in slightly damp annexes of the Adolescent Mental Health Unit and hate campaigns against the parent who makes you meals and arranges time off work to take you to appointments where you refuse to get out of the car and refuse to speak to anyone or even once dramatically tear up the meal plan and eat the strips of paper in front of them.

But I can definitely remember the first moment I noticed I was hungry, and it was the smell of the old kitchen that made me look for food. I don't care what the doctors called it. I called it homesickness.

I forgave Edward for not telling me about my brother. Eventually. He said they had always meant to tell me, when I was older. But then there was so much loss, he didn't know how to add another death. And it was my mother's call, her choice when to say something. Without her, he was never sure. It was something he still wanted her to decide. Even though now she couldn't.

The only thing he ever hinted about Emily's mother knowing his secrets was when I started work in a bookshop after college, and was talking too much about one of the owners. 'This is the one piece of advice I'll give you about work, Marianne: don't sleep with your boss. Believe me.'

I asked him if we could have a little gravestone for my missing brother, a place to decorate at the Wakes, so no one would forget him. Not hidden at the old Green Chapel on the river where no one would see it, but right there in the churchyard where I could cut rushes and lay down flowers. I was thinking perhaps if my mother came back she would be pleased with us for remembering my lost brother.

I asked about putting the 'Green Gravel' song on the stone, but he said, 'Have you any idea how much you pay per letter?' so we compromised with a tiny carved angel over his name. And if she didn't come back alive, at least now we had a place to go to remember her, and a place to bury her, next to his name.

14

The Owl Was a Baker's Daughter

Lady, baby, gypsy, queen,
Elephant, monkey, tangerine.

The boys called him AJ but girls had to say his name in full, Arthur Jack. I wanted to make his name last. I liked to trace its progress around my mouth, from the back of my throat to the half-smile it ended on. He wore his black hair half over his face and looked at us sideways from under his fringe.

Nearly every week the tattoo from his shoulder grew further down his arm, a tangle of dragons and snakes and vines and evil spirits peering out from the trees. He was too young for a tattoo, but that didn't stop him.

When he arrived at the Exclusion Unit in the morning he peeled his sweatshirt over his head, then pulled his T-shirt back over his shoulder and unwrapped whichever part of the tattoo was newest from its antiseptic clingfilm wrapping, and applied creams and oils. If you were the one sitting next to him, you were allowed to join in.

When he had oiled and caressed his impossibly beautiful arm and wrapped it up again and put his clothes back on in agonising slow motion, he would unwrap the arm of whichever of us girls was sitting next to him, and gently rub almond oil on the soft white insides of our arms.

We took it in turns to sit next to him. No one discussed this. We just did. And he never showed any reaction to any one of us, no sign of preference or attempt to communicate with one of us in particular. There was no competition for him. He was unavailable.

He had already been promised to Josie, who also lived on the travellers' site, and as soon as they both turned sixteen they would be married. She was still fourteen at this point, a round-faced girl with pale ginger plaits and invisible eyelashes, dressed in sequinned jeans and crop top, her little round child's belly sticking out in the middle.

Josie didn't go to school, so sometimes she would meet us in the park at lunchtime, or in the shopping arcade. She showed me pictures of the clothes she was wearing to a massive wedding party, and offered to try and do something with my hair. She thought I must have had some terrible accident to have such short hair.

I asked her why she didn't go to school, and she said she really didn't need it. And besides, there was so much work to do at home, she didn't have the time. It was odd, my outrage at this. I had spent all my school years up to this point failing to turn up and deriding it, claiming it was pointless, but faced with someone my age who simply did not attend, I was suddenly passionate about her right to be there.

Josie explained that in secondary school, or so she had heard, girls went with boys, and even had sex sometimes, and if she got into any of that it would break her father's heart. I could hardly argue with this. I had pretty much done exactly that. Girls in secondary schools, she'd heard, had no morals. They didn't even believe in God.

Purity was everything. At Christmas, Josie told me, every one of her brothers and sisters would get a new set of clothes, and not a stitch of it could have been on any other person, ever. Not a one. All the children had the same, down to the last sock and shoe. Pristine. Spotless. Pure.

Arthur Jack arrived late one time and said his auntie's dog had had puppies again. On the bloody laundry. Only three of them this time, and one was a runt and it was half-dead already. So he had to wait till one of the girls found him another shirt and ironed it for him. So it wasn't his fault he was late, was it?

I saw my opportunity. Casually, without making it sound like a big deal, handing him a cigarette along the park bench at lunchtime, I mentioned my dad was looking for a dog. Not me. That would have been too personal, too needy. That would never have worked. He looked away from me and blew a smoke ring. I knew better than to repeat the words. After he'd taken a last drag and flattened the stub on the back of the bench, he flipped his head back and stretched his arms into the air.

'Yeah, well, if you wankers want one of them pups I better tell them at home not to drown them all. They're right ugly little fuckers. Welcome to the lot of them.'

I laughed along with everyone else, not too loud, not first, just enough. In case a sudden movement might break the spell. I knew if the pups lived another week or so I could drop the next question into a conversation.

'So, when can I come and pick out one of the pups for my dad, then?'

And then I would be getting on to his bus and walking up the lane and actually going home with Arthur Jack, and taking a small creature from his arms and keeping it with me forever.

I was prepared to wait, and look away, and wait some more, and say nothing, and count down the days till those puppies were exactly eight weeks old when I would wrap one of them in an old towel and carry him or her home with me. At which point I would presumably have to confess to Edward that we now had a dog. Except I had not thought that far.

I had only thought as far as the moment when I would walk into the gates of the site, alongside Arthur Jack. When it happened I had that strange light-headedness you get when a plan works. I followed him down the lane from the bus stop to the travellers' site, a few steps behind him all the way while he blew smoke casually into the air above his head and kicked at occasional litter on the verge. I loved every minute. I did a trick I had of pinching my wrist very tight until I had a blood blister so that I would have a marker to remember every second of it.

I followed Arthur Jack through a high metal double gate, across a huge yard, collecting a little group of dogs following at my heels along the way. I looked at the dogs, wondering if one of them might be the mother of my puppy. Many of them were missing some aspect of their anatomy – an ear, an eye, a leg, a tail. I wondered if my puppy had survived with all its parts intact. Up to this point I hadn't bothered to ask much about it. Arthur Jack had shown a photograph of them all swarming together in a heap, impossible to tell which of them were black or brown or speckled or dappled or whatever the correct word is for dogs, and I had never asked for any more. I didn't dare ask too much or show too much interest in case my whole scheme went up in smoke.

All around the edge of the yard were static caravans and huge caravans you can pull behind a lorry or a big car, and occasional little wooden sheds. And in the middle were cars. A lot of cars. Some with no wheels. Some with no doors. Some really shiny new ones. All tangled together and parked like crazy paving. And crawling out from under and around them were children. Lots of children. It probably looked to me like a lot because they all stood still and stared at me. Two boys about Joe's age stopped kicking a very flat-looking football repeatedly at a tower of bricks that a car was resting on to watch me walk by. This was no ordinary car, either. It was a pale pink Cadillac with silver trim. I scampered up behind Arthur Jack.

'Do you think they're safe?' I said. 'Those boys? Should we stop them doing that?' He shook his head sadly and looked at his phone.

'I timed you. Fifty-five seconds from the gate before you started talking like a fucking social worker.' He pointed me in the direction of a small wooden house, and headed over in the opposite direction to join a group of young men sitting on crates at the side of a caravan.

I knocked on the door, and waited while a girl of about twelve opened the door and stared at me with her mouth open. An older woman behind her shouted something, but she just stood there.

'I'm Marianne, I met Arthur Jack at school. I've come for one of the puppies.' The older woman came to the door, and moved the girl to one side by her shoulders, then moved me in.

A very old woman who was curved into a half-moon sat perched on a wooden kitchen chair, shouting very loudly at another woman who was browning a huge pot of mince over a double gas boiler bolted onto a kitchen worktop. Two teenagers stood chopping carrots on either side of her, and behind the girls three babies sat strapped into car seats, two of them in full Aston Villa football kits – I had no idea you could get football kits that tiny – and a third one in a pink Babygro with her wisp of bright gold hair pulled into a silver scrunchy on top of her head.

The ancient, curved woman on the kitchen chair kept up a steady stream of talking, but it was so fast and musical and repetitive it took me a minute to recognise it as English.

I wondered if they had even noticed I was there. But then I began to understand some of what she was saying, and I realised they were saying Arthur Jack should have warned them, that they hadn't got anything good for supper, what would the girl think of them, and why was no one making the girl a cup of tea? One of the girls stopped chopping carrots and turned around to smile at me. It was Josie. But her smile was a very brief, secretive one, so I didn't say her name, in case there was some reason why she shouldn't have been friends with me already. She went to put on the kettle. There was some commotion at one of the windows, and one of the other girls took a box out from under the worktop and started taking out mugs.

Men's arms came in through the window. Wide brown

freckled arms with tattoos of the Virgin Mary or lists of names. A bag of sugar came out of another box, and was spooned into the cups with a dessert spoon until all the mugs of tea had disappeared out of the window.

The old woman smiled at me. I drank my tea standing in the middle of the room, grinning at them all, bobbing down and grinning at the babies in their car seats, too, playing peekaboo from around my mug. Sugar was one of the many foods I refused at the time, but I remember enjoying every drop of that mug of sweet tea. The old woman held out her beautiful long brown twisted hands to me, and I held them. Her rings and silver bracelets were loose on her knobbly fingers and stringy wrists.

She said, 'See, the boy found this sweet girl to have one of our pups. This kind girl. See, what a nice girl he brought us. A good-hearted girl, see how she holds my hand, smiles at the babies. God love her.'

I had not been called sweet, or nice, or good for such a long time. Perhaps it had been my mother who last said all those words about me, a lifetime, a world, a universe ago. Perhaps they are words that only mothers say. Or perhaps these women saw something in me everyone else had long forgotten. Because they were purely mother, grandmother, and saw me as purely girl. Nothing more complicated.

The old woman kept holding on to my hands, and stroking the rough patches on my knuckles. She reached up and stroked my short, patchy hair too. Sometimes I understood what she said, sometimes the other woman at the cooking pot told me what she said, and I understood she was her grandmother, and stone deaf, and to keep smiling at her. I did.

When the mince was browned and the carrots cooked, the girls ladled it into a dozen or more cereal bowls, and opened the other door, which led to a bedroom, and shouted a list of names into the bedroom where a huge TV was attached to one wall. What seemed to me a swarm of boys appeared from the bedroom or the window or the doorway and collected a bowl of mince each and a spoon and a piece of bread and butter. Meat was another food I was refusing, but I found myself happily dipping the bread into the gravy and letting the butter drip onto my hand as I scooped it up along with the rest of them.

The younger children were lined up at a basin of hot water and had their faces and hands scraped clean with a pile of flannel pieces. Then they sat down to eat. Along two walls of the main kitchen room were narrow mattresses on the floor covered in different patterned blankets, and the children sat in two long rows on them, with their legs straight out in front of them.

I sat with them, and asked them questions like, how old are you? Do you like carrots? Do you think they look like pennies? We could pretend we're eating money! Do you like drawing? Would you like me to do a drawing for you? I can do dogs, and horses, and cats. Which one would you like? What's your favourite colour? Do you like the puppies? Which one is the funniest? The most handsome?

They didn't reply, just nudged each other and giggled as if Arthur Jack had brought home a giraffe or a talking parrot. But every time I smiled and tried again the old woman nodded at me, and smiled and said, 'See, she's a sweet girl, we have to find her the best puppy. The very best one. She's a good girl, you can see, a kind girl, she'll have a beautiful baby of her own one day, look how lovely she is.'

I had hardly any hair, and dry skin from bad eating and smudged black make-up and ripped jeans and a black jumper I liked because it was huge and I could hide inside it and bring my knees right up to my chest, but I sat there believing I was lovely, kind, sweet, a good girl, who would have lovely babies just like these golden-haired ones. So I smiled and ate my mince and waited for Arthur Jack to bring in the box of puppies.

The mother did not sit down to eat. There was nowhere for her to sit, and no time either. As she collected up the bowls and told the children to eat the rest of their bread and wiped the spills from the floor and shook out the blankets and laid them back straight, she went back to the big pan from time to time and had a spoonful of food. Then she scraped it out and ate what was left, and started washing it up.

The girls had fetched washing up bowls of water from somewhere else. I offered to help, but they said no, they had a way of doing it, and I could see it was a lot more thorough than what we did at home. There was a system, and a row of bowls to wash once, wash again, rinse, then stack. Then they used the rinsing bowl to wash out the dishcloths and hung them on a line over the window. One of them went outside to find all the mugs the men had taken out before, and wash them, and start all over again with the teas.

The grandmother didn't let me move far, or do anything to help. She kept hold of my hand, or stroked my hair, or talked to me in a jumbled sing-song. She said her sister Margaret had taken like that, when their mother died, had gone into black like me, torn her clothes, cut her hair off, it was a terrible thing.

Terrible. She had cut her skin, and stopped eating properly. She was such a kind-hearted girl. It takes them the worst, and her so young. Now look at her, she was lucky, she had lived so long all these were her great-grandchildren, and one of them now expecting her first, pray God it will be a kind-hearted girl for her, don't let the men hear me say that, they all want boys, but a woman needs a girl like this one, to keep close to her. And it falls hardest for them. I tried to tell her that was my mother's name, Margaret, and when the others said, 'She can't hear,' I tried to spell it out, and write it down, and the mother said she didn't know any of that reading or writing stuff.

I didn't try to tell her it was nine years since my mother went, that I hadn't worn black all that time, or always cut my hair off, or torn my clothes and my skin, or that everyone was wearing ripped denim that year. I accepted her version gratefully. I was in mourning for my mother. I was a kind-hearted girl, the kind every mother needs, and they always take it the hardest. She told me she would pray for me. She told me to eat my food, and pray, and trust to God that when my babies came there would be a girl for me, and I would put my sorrow aside like her sister did after her babies came, God love her, she was kind-hearted all her life till she was taken back to God, and every one of them missed her still.

Another grown-up boy came out of the dark bedroom and all the women shouted at him for missing supper. He rolled a cigarette on the kitchen side and asked for a cup of tea, and some bread and sugar if that was all they had left.

An older man came and stood in the doorway. He said he had come to talk to me.

'Now,' he said, 'I hear from Arthur Jack that you're a fair

hand at reading and all that business. A fair hand at it all.' I didn't deny it. He settled into the door frame, blowing cigarette smoke carefully outside away from the babies. He comfortably filled the doorway, one enormous arm leaning across the lintel.

'Well, you see, if you can read all them papers, you'll know. There's a thing bothering me, and I can't make it out. Not without the reading. It's that fellow who's got the airplanes and trains and so forth, Mr Branson. Now I've been hearing he's buying up a parcel of land over where there used to be an airstrip, not one that's used now, and you cannot buy land round there for any money. I know, cos I tried. And it's to do with him building a new airfield, see, where you can't hear the noise of it. And if a person were to buy a bit of land round about there, maybe a bit of woodland or something no one wants, they might stand to make a bit of money on it, when that fellow comes round needing to buy it all up.'

I said I hadn't read anything about it.

'Not a thing about it,' he said. 'I see. Makes a man wonder, that. How he keeps it all out of the papers.' I said I would ask my father. He knew a lot more than I did. This seemed to appease him.

Then he said, 'That Arthur Jack, my sister's boy. He's been sent to school now, so he can do the reading, make sure of what they put down in contracts and so forth. Like the problem with this house, you see. If we had read the papers. We got the windows wrong, and now we have to take it down and do it again.'

'But where will you go?'

'Oh, there's the static caravans, the women prefer them anyway. It's just, if we want to build on this land, we have to start with one of these, see, then ask to build a house.' I didn't see at all, but I nodded.

'So, my sister's boy. Is he doing well? Is he top of the class there at that school of yours?' It occurred to me that allowing Arthur Jack to go to the Exclusion Unit instead of working at home with his uncle might be a concession, so I said, 'Yes, he's very clever. He'll do really well.'

'He won't be doing any of those exams, mind. We don't want him turning into an idiot.' He turned round then and walked away. I had no idea what to say to that. Hardly anyone at the unit was doing exams. Edward was furious about it. It was the reason behind many angry phone calls in our house. It had never occurred to me anyone would see exams as a way to make their children unnecessarily stupid. But then I hadn't done any exams myself. I didn't know.

It was dark by now, so Josie was sent to get Arthur Jack to fetch the puppies, but he sent a message back with her for us to do it ourselves. So Josie took the other girl with her and between them they carried in a cardboard box of puppies. The mother dog followed her as far as the doorway, then waited. One of the mother dog's ears was half-missing. Other than that she was a nice enough looking dog, something like a smaller Labrador shape, with a pale brown coat.

The puppies had not inherited their mother's good looks. Their heads were too wide for their bodies, and their ears were too big for their heads. Their little tails were ratty worm-like things. Their eyes were bulging, their feet were flat and fluffy, and none of them had a coat that was all of one piece. They looked as if they had dressed themselves out of the dressing up box where all the children were fighting over a few suits of clothes. The smallest of the three, who I guessed must be the runt that Arthur Jack had promised would not live, had a face half-white and half-black, one blue eye and one brown, as if he had been the last to rummage at the bottom of the box for something to wear.

When I picked him up the woman who'd been in charge of cooking said, 'Now, Marianne, you don't want to bother with the runt. Michael should have done away with it weeks ago. It's only got the one eye that works, God help it.'

They had called me kind, and sweet, and lovely. They kept saying God love her. God love her. So I took the runt. They wrapped him in a towel, and I carried him home inside my jumper. There was plenty of room in there. He peed all down my belly while I sat at the bus stop, and whimpered and cried all the way home. It was a long journey. Two buses and a long walk at either end. My arms ached and I was afraid someone would see him and make me get off the bus. I was afraid I would drop him, or he would wriggle out of my clothes and fall to the ground.

When I got him home, Edward was out at Joe's parents' evening, and I was at a loss what to give the puppy to eat. Was he old enough for meat? Was cow's milk safe for dogs? There wasn't much in the fridge. Eggs? Do dogs eat eggs? I didn't know. Already my stomach was covered in flea bites. I didn't have a bed for him, or a collar or a bowl or even anything to put in it. I had only thought as far as bringing him back to Edward. Then everything would be alright.

I didn't want to put the puppy down anywhere, so I kept him inside my jumper and walked around with him. When the towel was too wet and dirty I changed it for another. And when they still had not come home after an hour I gave the puppy some water and wrapped him in another towel and took him to my bed.

I heard them coming home, happy, sharing fish and chips and congratulations, and I decided not to wake the puppy by going downstairs. I remembered then I had promised to babysit that night so Edward could go to the school. But now he'd had to take Joe with him, and keep him out late. I remembered him writing it on the calendar on the kitchen wall, and circling it, and reminding me, and I realised he might still be angry with me for forgetting. I also knew that by the morning he would only talk to me gently about it, and that I didn't deserve his gentleness.

I lay in bed ashamed of myself, ashamed of the kind words I had accepted all evening, like the sweetness and kindness and good-heartedness Edward kept taking on trust, and that I kept failing to show him. I called out goodnight from behind my bedroom door, careful to keep the tears out of my voice, and curled around that ugly little dog to comfort him in his homesickness and cried into his coat for my uselessness. Which is how he got the name Teddy.

I was downstairs unusually early the next morning, driven from my bed by puppy mess and flea bites and whimpering. I could hear Edward and Joe in the kitchen making their packed lunches. There was some kind of negotiation going on to do with cheese, and they didn't do much more than glance at the puppy. I took this as a good sign. And it seemed Edward had got the memo about me being a sweet girl who took it all to heart, because he didn't mention the babysitting or the dog, except to say, 'So you've got a dog now?' which I took as permission granted. If he had said, 'we've got a dog,' or, worse still, 'I,' then it would have meant I was in trouble, and Teddy was probably on his way to a pet shop. He backed out of the door with his work bag and coat and Joe's lunch box and book folder and two unmatched gloves and a permission slip letter and the car keys, then put it all down on the porch and came back into the hall.

He took a good look at the puppy then, holding its head gently in both hands, and frowning at his blank blue eye. 'Look in the yellow pages for a vet if you're keeping him, Marianne. I'll bring you a book on how to look after him.'

And he did bring me the book, and to his great surprise I read it, and signed up for puppy training and held down a Saturday job to pay for it all. And Edward took him to the vet's and spoke to him gently and calmly and cleaned up after him in the kitchen, and never said anything more critical than 'It's not the worst thing you could have done, you know, bringing home that dog.'

I missed quite a bit of schooling staying home to train Teddy and look after him, but no more than I had missed before he came along, and now when I was at home all day I had company. And when my key worker came on a home visit we spent the whole time talking about Teddy and playing with him and she took photos of the blanket I had sewn with his name, and said to Edward what a good idea it was of his, to get me a puppy. How therapeutic. Edward shrugged. I let him have that one. And in Teddy's one good eye I remained a good, sweet, kind-hearted girl.

From time to time I would take in a photo of Teddy to show my classmates at the Exclusion Unit, but Arthur Jack never showed any interest. I asked if I could bring the puppy back to show his grandmother how he had turned out, but he only shrugged and turned away. I was never invited back.

I knew all along I had chosen the right dog. Not because he turned out to be so loyal and sweet and he was the perfect excuse to do my university years from home, which was just as well for a basket case like me, not because he made me take walks and hold down a Saturday job to pay for his food, nor that he kept me company all through my twenties, all the way through to just before Susannah was born, when he seemed to realise I didn't need him quite as badly, and quietly died in his sleep.

But because I was well versed in fairy tales I knew that given the choice of three, the first gold, the second silver, the third plain wood, you should always choose the plainest, smallest third out of any set of three. Three brothers, three sisters, three caskets of treasure. You pick the least assuming, and make sure you thank everyone who helped you on your way. Especially if one of them is an old woman. An old woman with beautiful long fingers covered in jewels who cannot hear you but knows you for who you are.

You should learn from the owl, who used to be a baker's daughter, to be especially kind and polite to an old woman, because if you refuse her food or small kindnesses, she will turn you into a creature of the night condemned to shout out for help and for no one to understand what you are saying. You will cry your owl's cry into the night forever and no one will comfort you.

15

Practising Pagan

Hinx, minx, the old witch winks
The fat begins to fry.
Nobody home but jumping Joan
Father, Mother and I.

Stick stock, stone dead
Blind man can't see.
Every knave shall have a slave
You or I must be HE!

In my second year at art school a visiting lecturer called Mark was really kind to me and showed a lot of interest in my work. I was painting scenes from the ballad 'Tam Lin', I remember, using a mixture of chalk, charcoal and glue. The results were strangely lumpy and unconvincing. Janet looked like one of those Soviet land girls on posters, all muscle and determination. He asked why I had painted Tam Lin himself so pale and chalky and thin. What was that about? Was he supposed to look so ill? I had always thought of Tam Lin as green, I don't know why. Like the green children in my mother's story, perhaps.

I said I thought he had lived so long a captive in fairyland that they had only been feeding him grass. Everyone knows you shouldn't eat their food.

'Hmm yes,' he said, 'I know those stories too. But yours still looks a bit poorly to me.' Good point. Next to the Stakhanovite Janet he was a weak and insubstantial creature, clearly in need of rescuing. 'It looks like Janet is the hero of your version,' he said.

'Well, isn't she? She has to hold on to a lion and a snake before the queen lets Tam Lin go, and even then she has to live with the curse: *Woe betide her ill-starred face, an ill death may she die!* You'd have to be a strong person to take that on the chin.'

He asked a lot of questions about the ballads themselves, especially the ones with transmigration of the soul. I was pleased someone was finally interested in that idea. After he left I got his written feedback on my work, and he said how he had enjoyed seeing 'the work of a practising pagan'.

Was that me? I had no idea I was any kind of pagan. And I have always been very bad at practising anything. As in doing anything regularly and with intent. Unfortunately he had left by then, as visitors only stayed one term, so I couldn't ask what he meant. Except I knew it meant me. By extension it must also have meant my mother.

At the end of the summer term he came back to give us a lecture on his own work, and to see our summer show. His own work was tiny brightly coloured paintings on copper discs that seemed to glow like lit abstracts until you got up close and saw they were made up of tiny people and trees and animals all random sizes dancing about. He had painted them all in single hair brushes. Each piece was no bigger than a saucer.

He asked to see my section of the summer exhibition, and congratulated me on my grade. My entire exhibition was made up of illustrations of *Pearl*. I had assumed it would fail because I never managed to illustrate the entire story, but then none of the art department had read it anyway, so they gave me a distinction.

I had made the paintings out of found objects: seed heads, acorns, litter, pieces of Kinder Surprise toys, sweet wrappers, fragments of children's books ripped into strips all built on a map of our old village. It was perhaps my first serious attempt to draw the whole story, a serious upgrade on the coloured pencil drawings in school exercise books or the black-and-white photographs I had used in my foundation year show.

But I had only really shown the start and end to the story. I had the walled garden, the herb beds, the child's grave, the walk to the river, and the dreamer waking on the grave. The whole episode at the riverbank where he talks to his dead child was represented by a strip of shiny blue plastic rope I found by the canal, stitched along the edge of some frames. The banks of angels had evaporated into a reflection of a cathedral upside down in a sort of sweet-wrapper pond.

I had imagined it as a perfect circle, a string of beads with tiny clues linking each to the next like neat clips holding together the links in a string of rosary beads. But somehow I became obsessed with each painting, balancing one set of plastic legs with another doll's hand, painting layer after layer of acrylic, searching for the perfect way to make the dirty water of the ponds look deeper in the middle, the mud more broken and shiny at the edges. Most of the words from the picture books were lost under paint and glue and fragments of pottery.

I thought that if I made each painting as beautiful as I could, then the whole story would reveal itself when they were assembled, as if some kind of magic were involved. But when I put them in a row all I saw was confusion, uneven surfaces, rough edges, the story lost, the meaning, whatever it was, not revealed to me, but hidden further and further from my sight with each coat of paint and glue and varnish.

And where was the pearl? I had embedded a pearl-like piece of plastic jewellery along with a doll's silver high-heeled slipper somewhere in the first garden. But once I moved the paintings from the studio to the exhibition hall I couldn't see them. Perhaps I had put them back in the wrong order. Somehow the grave had moved to the end. Or the pearl had fallen off somewhere, or been painted over by mistake.

I went back along the corridors searching in the rough wooden trolleys we had used to move our work. Perhaps someone else had used that trolley after me. I rummaged through the shavings and dust and soft red clay in the bottom of the trolley, looking for my lost toys. I walked along the corridors kicking at the clay-coloured mess pushed against the skirting boards all the way to the studio that was already dismantled, the dividing walls pushed back and the masking tape and edges of odd pieces of paper pulled from the walls into a rough pile in the middle under a huge skylight.

The room was oddly light and echoey without the partitions. Someone was mixing a giant tub of white emulsion using a massive electric whisk thing, and everyone else was shouting above the noise. Two people had already started whitewashing the back wall, dripping badly mixed paint across the floor, and other people were grabbing the brushes and shrieking as the paint flew in all directions. I could barely tell where my workspace used to be. I wouldn't find anything in there.

I headed out of the art school to a charity shop a few streets over, where I often found useful objects. Perhaps they had some cheap jewellery. But I got distracted by a set of breakfast bowls and a terrible green velvet cloak I wished I'd had when I was painting Tam Lin, and eventually wandered back to the art school with a board game from the 1970s called Magic Robot.

There were two circles inside the box. You pointed a magnetic robot at a question in the first circle and then placed him on the other side of the board, where he spun around until his wire wand pointed to the answer. There were several circles of questions and answers to choose from, and you had to line up the right circle of questions with its matching answers, or you got nonsense.

By the time I got back to the art school with a Magic Robot instead of lunch I had missed a lot of the cleaning up and my tutor had already rearranged my long line of depressing *Pearl* collages into a square of thirty-six, with a pile of rejected ones stacked on the floor. The new arrangement was based on a balance of colours and textures, the detail at eye level fading out into the corners. I had to admit it looked a lot better.

But any connection to the story, to a sequence of events, was utterly destroyed. I can't remember if the one with the missing pearl even made it to the wall. I had lost patience with its garish colours and indistinct faces. Out of sheer anger I stuck the Magic Robot somewhere near the middle, surrounded by questions about square and cube numbers, his answers to art and nature and space dotted about the outer edges. The robot was apparently a key factor in my distinction.

By the time we got to the opening night, I hated it. I would have taken it down if I'd had anything better to put in its place. After Mark had finished his talk and packed away his work, I hid in a corner of the canteen too ashamed to talk to him about what I had on the walls. But he searched through the whole building until he found me. His wife Marie had come with him especially to meet me, he said.

'I've been telling her about your work,' he said. 'She's gone over to the hall to track it down.' We had to go up two flights of stairs from the canteen to the exhibition, and Mark had to stop and catch his breath on each landing.

'Do you like German cakes?' he said. 'Marie is German, and I've promised her a trip to the German bakery – would you like to come? They have the most amazing Sachertorte! If you don't know what it is, you definitely have to come!'

I spotted Marie standing in front of my *Pearl* collages, a short round woman with hennaed red hair falling out of a bun on the top of her head, dressed in a long skirt with suns and moons on it and a bright turquoise jumper. She was so enthusiastic when she spoke she sort of bounced onto the balls of her red suede trainers. Embarrassingly, she was mostly enthusing about the Magic Robot.

'Mark told me about your collages! He said they were very witty. Witty? Do I mean witty? They're wonderful. I love the robot! He's my favourite! The questions about numbers! And a square of six by six! You must know about numerology as well. No?'

'I started off with lots more. I'm not sure where they went.'

'But choosing the right ones is part of the process!'

'Well, I think my tutor did that. Is six a good number? Or thirty-six?'

'It's perfect! Look at the squares inside the square! Each quarter section is like a little story inside the story, see?'

'It would be a whole lot more impressive if I'd known what I was doing!'

'Nonsense, you were using instincts. Well-trained instincts!'

'And quite a bit of lucky dip in the nearest Oxfam shop.'

No matter how I tried to explain that I was no kind of pagan and hardly any kind of artist, Mark and Marie listened as if I made perfect sense, as if I might even know what was happening in the pictures. They also insisted on taking me to the German cake shop and introducing me to Sachertorte. I began to think maybe they did want to get to know me, even if they were sadly deluded about my talents.

They invited me to a summer barbecue at their house that Saturday afternoon, said all the neighbours always came along. They called it some kind of special word, and I was worried that meant I was supposed to bring along a particular kind of food or drink. I wondered if it was a German word. I wasn't sure I'd heard it correctly, so I asked what I should bring. 'Absolutely nothing,' they said. 'Just bring yourself!' I blushed.

It didn't seem likely to me that my own self was a good addition to any kind of party, especially if I turned up with no food or drink, so I spent Saturday morning making a chocolate cheesecake, helping myself to one of Edward's bottles of white wine, and ironing a summer dress two sizes too big for me that I had found in a charity shop and had always intended to cut up and make into something better.

Their address was in the vast 1930s housing estate next to the park where Joe liked to sail his toy boats and where I always got lost, so I set off from the bus station with the cheesecake on a plate covered in silver foil in one hand and an A–Z of Birmingham in the other. I felt awkward in the dress, which bunched around the waist, and was dangerously pale for anyone carrying a chocolate cheesecake on a hot day. I wished I had worn my usual jeans and a T-shirt. Once I set off across the park I was instantly lost, even with an A–Z, and it didn't help that I had to keep sitting on a bench to put the plate down and try to read the right page.

I was sitting on a park bench turning the A–Z round and round in my hands trying to work out which direction I was facing, when a young man pushing a bicycle stopped in front of me.

'Marianne? What are you doing here? Are you going to church or something?' I recognised him from art school, one of the impossibly cool boys who only wore black and had perfect skin. They were all called Ben or Dan or something snappy. I think this was one of the Bens. Even his bicycle was black and polished and gleaming in the sun. I assumed his comment about church was because of the dress. So I knew it was a mistake. It didn't help that I was wearing a long-sleeved T-shirt underneath it to cover the scars on my arms, or that the ancient buttons down the front fell out of their ancient worn buttonholes every few steps.

'I'm supposed to be at a summer barbecue. Only I'm late. And lost.' I told him the name of the street, and he doubled over his crossbar with laughter.

'A summer SOLSTICE barbecue! Where they take all their clothes off and do chanting? Yeah, I'll show you the way. All the streets on that side are full of them. Witches. Druids. You know? Crystals hanging in the front window. Vegan pie.' I picked up my cheesecake and A–Z and followed him out of the park. I didn't have time to stop and keep rebuttoning my dress because he walked quite fast. From time to time he looked over at me and laughed again.

'No really, you'll fit in fine. What's that you've got? Lentil bake? Jeez! Wait till I tell Dan. It'd better be organic and sugarfree. Sure you still want to go?' He stopped by an overgrown front garden where the bow window was, as he predicted, hung with a large collection of crystals.

'Thanks for the directions. Well, for showing me the way.'

'Don't say I didn't warn you. Go home by nine or they all take their clothes off.' He jumped on the bike in one smooth motion, and took the corner at a perfect angle. I probably imagined him giggling as he did so; he must have been too far away by then for me to hear.

The front door was wide open, and I could hear the sounds of children in the back garden, a layer of women's voices chatting, a bass line of further distant men. The hallway smelled of fresh mint, and old wood, and new bread. Perhaps Mark was right about my mother being a pagan, if this is what a pagan house smelled like. Along the wall under the stairs were two broomsticks, their handles decorated with dried flowers. Marie came out of the kitchen.

'Marianne! You came! And look, you've brought pudding. You will be popular! I'll pop it in the freezer for a few minutes to revive it. Do you like our broomsticks? Sentimental, I know. These were the ones we used for our wedding ceremony, you know, as in Jump the Broomstick?'

I followed her into the kitchen where all her friends were dressed in long dresses and had hennaed hair down to their waists. The kitchen was full of them, broad hips pressed from table to countertop to fridge, while their wide freckled arms unwrapped salads and chopped things and threaded mushrooms and peppers onto kebab sticks and poured drinks and handed mugs of home-brewed beer out of the open door.

They all talked at once and told each other to stop, and laughed, and carried on. I was smoothed and petted and questioned and handed a glass of my mother's iced tea complete with sprig of mint and a slice of lemon. I hardly dared drink it in case I broke the spell.

One of them said, 'Oh you are the girl with the ballad paintings, aren't you? Mark told us about them. Have you got a website?' One of them admired the material of my dress, and I remembered that was why I had bought it, the strange blue-green geometric pattern, the scalloped edge to the hem. I said yes, I'd found it in a charity shop and never got round to remaking it. The buttons were always coming undone.

'Oh, sew up the front, I would. Then you could keep them. Look, they're handmade, like the dress. It's only the sleeves that are worn. You could take them off, like a sort of pinafore.' Marie shooed them away like friendly chickens.

'Leave the girl alone. You'll frighten her off. It looks fine as it is, Marianne, come through to the garden and I'll find you some shade.'

The garden was full of pergolas and improvised shade made of colourful drapes between runner bean trees and random collections of rugs and chairs where people were sitting and chatting and drinking tall drinks or tipping back beer bottles, and children lay on the rugs or ran between the wooden beds or pulled ice cubes out of their drinks and threw them at each other.

There were herb beds and vegetable beds my mother would have loved, raised beds with ingenious arrangements for collecting rainwater, every kind of recycled container was sprouting something you could eat or which smelled good. One whole side of the garage was dotted with giant yogurt pots painted in bright stripes and geraniums growing out of them. Beneath them a row of tomatoes was growing in assorted sinks, crates and a toilet bowl. The smell along the wall, of warm geranium and tomato leaves, was dense and oily and familiar. I recognised the greenhouse smell from behind our old washhouse.

I asked Marie, 'Do tomatoes and geraniums like to grow together? I think my mother used to put them together.'

'It's not so much they like to be together as the greenfly don't like the geraniums, and they like the tomatoes a bit too much. Or that's the idea.' Marie flicked a tomato leaf and greenfly fell into her palm. 'See?'

All along the end of the garden was a wooden chalet painted bright blue with bright yellow double doors opening on to a veranda hung with disco balls and twisted metal rods that spun gently, reflecting the colours of the shed and the garden.

Marie said, 'Come on, let me show you my shed. It took all last winter to build it, and I love to show it off!' She pushed open the yellow double doors, and I could see why she wanted to show it off. There was a whole wall covered in drawer units from an old draper's shop, drawers with little glass windows in them, still labelled things like gloves – plain and ribbon – green, though I could see each one was full of different paints or chalks or pencils. A long workbench under the window had a row of syrup and treacle tins with different pens and pieces of shiny equipment she said she used for silversmithing.

Marie told me she taught evening classes in how to make jewellery. She said any time I felt like coming along, she would give me a free session. In the summer she sometimes held day classes, where you came home with a set of rings or earrings each time. She picked out a pair of earrings she had been working on, to show me how they were made – a crescent moon, then two tiny discs of silver hanging on silver chains. She said they would look really good on me with my short hair. She wrapped them in tissue and pressed them into my hand.

Then she opened a series of tiny wooden drawers built into the desk, and took out a wooden dowel with a flat-head screw in the top and a pair of pliers, and showed me how to bend the silver circles open then shut, to make a chain. I made a simple set of rings, and fixed them into the lowest hole in my ears and she said, 'You look beautiful!' I knew I wasn't.

I felt desperately awkward all of a sudden, aware of my faded dress and trainers, the itch of cuts on my arms, the cold patches where my hair doesn't grow in properly over my ears. I looked around for the exit before I started to cry. Something about her gesture of handing me a home-made gift, and telling me I looked beautiful in it, must have brought my mother back to me, that and the smell of geraniums and tomato leaves in the summer garden.

I was thinking of my last jumper with the differently striped sleeves, the clink and jingle of the beads along the cuffs before I chewed the threads, but worse than that, the clean uncut skin of my wrists beneath them. My mother smoothing my hair behind my ears, onions and garden on her fingertips, the backs of my ears smooth and plain and unencumbered with clips and hoops and scabs.

Marie pretended not to notice my tears, backed off, said, stay as long as you like, look around, join us in the garden when you're ready. When she left me alone in the workshop it still smelled of her, of red candles and new wood and camphor and the hot breath of the barbecue outside the window hanging in the air like an aftertaste of her soft oval-shaped vowel sounds and sing-song foreign voice.

I watched from the open doorway for a while. All the women were dressed in long colourful skirts except one very small older woman sitting under the best shade, her skin pale as milk under a long cream dress, her head shaved smooth, her eyelids coloured in bright green and gold. There were plenty of children, running along the narrow paths between raised beds and spraying each other with sprinklers and dragging watering cans half their size along woodchip paths or building little piles of woodchips then flattening them. One of the older children came to fetch me.

'Are you Marianne? Mark said you'd help us with the treasure hunt.' She held out her hot little hand to me and I took it, grateful for the easy way she gave me of walking back into the party. She turned my hand over, and stroked the marks on my wrist.

'What happened to your arm?'

'It got caught in some gooseberry bushes. In a different garden.

And maybe some blackberries too. Or thistles.'

'Are there any blackberries here?'

'No, this is a very safe treasure hunt. I think Mark cut down all the blackberry bushes specially.' I was aware as I said it of my mother's voice inside mine, her kind of explanations, the stories she told me, and I wondered, fleetingly, if she sometimes said them to me with tears in her eyes or scars on her arms, and I accepted them as easily as this little girl called Rose took my hand and led me through the garden.

By the time we had eaten all the vegetarian kebabs and the salads and drunk a lot of beer out of assorted mugs and teacups, Mark and most of the men had taken off their shirts, and started spraying all the hot little children with a garden hose, so before long they were all naked. There was no sudden stopping of the party and restarting with no clothes, the guests simply wore less and less as the evening set in.

For most, this was not a pretty sight. Mark was round and hairy in a tufted gingery way, but the other men were the knotty stringy middle-age that looks better in clothes no matter what the season. The very old lady with a shaved head folded her long pale dress neatly and laid it over her wicker chair so the seat would not be uncomfortable. Underneath she had a long pale petticoat with loose straps that showed two lines of scars from her armpits across her empty chest.

Some of the grown-ups asked if I would like to go and

babysit their children. They wrote their names and numbers on the unfolded lid of my cigarette packet. Rose made me a kind of giant daisy chain out of random flowers she had found in the garden. Perhaps there was a moment when I ought to have gone home, somewhere just after the hosing of the children and before the women stepped out of their dresses, but I had somehow missed it.

Then the women all remembered there was pudding. My cheesecake came out of the freezer like a slab of lava, there were fruit kebabs and sticky chocolate crispy cakes, and fairy cakes and fruit pies and jellies, all set out in the kitchen so they wouldn't melt.

By now there were several degrees of nakedness going on, and I would have gladly got rid of the inappropriate dress if I'd had something elegant on underneath. Something that covered all the marks of cutting on my thighs and my belly and, worst of all, on my arms. I'd like to tell you that I'd put all that nonsense behind me, that these were simply the signs and scars and ridges left behind from a sadder time, but some of those lines were fresh.

Tucked inside the lining of my cigarette packet was a fresh razor blade. I'd added a few new lines when I was alone in the workshop that afternoon. Sometimes I would reach for the blade and be surprised it was dirty, or be surprised to see there were fresh tracks on my legs. I didn't always remember doing it, the way you might not remember if you made your bed this morning, because it's something you always do.

As everyone moved towards the kitchen and the puddings only the old woman with no hair and I were left in the garden. I could feel the pulse in my arms under my T-shirt, the blood literally itching for a way out, as if the veins themselves were rising up visibly through the layer of white T-shirt and the soft blue-green patterns of the dress. As the first children wandered back under their shades with bowls of jelly and ice cream, I picked up my bag and headed out of the side gate, down the path and out onto the road.

It was only when I was back in the park that I realised I had left behind my cigarette packet with the secret razor blade, and the names and telephone numbers for babysitting. If they opened the packet and found the razor blade they wouldn't want me to look after their children anyway, but I was sorry this meant I wouldn't see them again.

Eventually I found my way back out of the main park gates and across town to the bus station, where I fidgeted and scratched and longed for a cigarette and wondered what my life would be like if I went to Saturday schools in silversmithing, and accepted gifts of silver and friendship from a kind, childless couple who showed every sign of liking me, and babysat their pagan friends' pagan children and maybe even became a real pagan myself who got married in a home-made ceremony where I jumped a broomstick and grew vegetables and made bread and retold my mother's stories to my cheerful pagan children.

But mostly I thought how my mother would have loved it there. She would have loved the garden, and the children too. She would have asked the grown-ups all about the herbs and the different watering systems and told the children riddles and funny rhymes. All the way home on the bus I could feel the warmth of her sitting next to me, and carried on one of my silent conversations with her about it. Sometimes I think I have lived my life as an observer, saving all the best bits for her by looking very carefully and trying to remember the details she would have liked.

Was my mother a practising pagan? I don't think so. She sang old songs. She talked to every living thing. To the tree before she broke its branches. To the roots hanging into the cave. To single magpies, obviously. Doesn't everyone? To the little people. If she lost her favourite trowel in the garden again she would say, 'Now where have you little menaces moved that trowel of mine?'

Similarly rats. Rats will leave your house if you ask them politely. 'Mr Rat,' she would say, 'I am sorry to trouble you when you are very busy, but you see it is very inconvenient your staying in our house at the moment. We would much prefer you to live in the barn, which you will find warm and suitable for your family. I hope you don't take it amiss. Thank you.' One time I said, but they aren't here right now. They come out at night. Should we write them a letter? She laughed. Rats can't read! Of course not. How silly of me.

She read the I Ching and the Old Testament. She read the Tao-te-Ching and folk tales. She blew into the nostrils of horses and cows, and spoke to them in a soft, even voice. She collected stories and songs and beliefs in the same way she collected empty jars for next year's damson jam or the colourful shards of crockery she dug from our ancient garden. For their usefulness, their colour, their history.

All the way home as I told her about the barbecue and the broomsticks and the home-made beer and the little knotty men and the hennaed women and the children in the sprinkler and the melted cheesecake she was cracking up with laughter. As I got off the bus in Wolverhampton I was still wiping the odd tear of laughter from my face and she said very clearly in my left ear, 'I cannot believe you didn't know the name for the summer solstice! You should have known to wear your best undies!'

My mother had an outrageous laugh. She laughed at things that, as a child, I couldn't see were funny, but when she laughed you had to join in too. It was a huge cracked-open explosion of laughter that often brought her to tears. She would shriek with laughter, out of all proportion. Sometimes when I am saving all the good bits of a bad day for her, or when I set out to do something slightly odd, I think I am trying to make her laugh. I hold up paintings that have gone badly wrong for her to laugh at them. I shrug at absurdities, looking up to hear her loud, childlike reaction. She loved terrible jokes, and it did not matter how often she had heard them, she still found them funny.

Most of all she liked stories where something ridiculous goes wrong. One day Edward got the car stuck in a flood on the way home. He was only just outside the village so he flagged someone down and together they pushed the car into the little petrol station and parked it at the side. He arrived home late with dark watermarks around his ankles and his feet making sloshing noises inside his shoes.

The next day he walked back to the garage and found he had parked it in the MOT testing area by mistake. The garage owner was a very eccentric man with shaggy black hair and a shaggy black dog called Pooh. He handed Edward a bill for an MOT. Edward said he wouldn't have minded so much, only the car had failed. My mother loved that story.

16

Where Babies Come From

Raspberry, strawberry, gooseberry jam,
Tell me the name of your young man!
A – *B* – C – *D* – E – *F* – G

I knew all along they came out of your mother. When my mother was pregnant with Joe she had a game where each month I had to find an object in the house the size of the baby. A peach pit. A plum. An apple. A grapefruit. Besides, I could see him getting bigger, watch him turn over like a duck's back rising as it dipped its head under water. I knew when they went off to the hospital and Mrs Wynne came to babysit all night that the next day they would come back with a whole new person. No one was telling me any nonsense about gooseberry bushes.

At primary school there was a lot of talk about the baby stuff. When we hung upside down by our knees from the climbing bars with our skirts falling over our faces, we liked to stay hanging there so long we could make farting noises with our vaginas. We hung there with our school skirts falling over our heads, letting air in and pushing it out, and talking about what fingers we could put in the hole.

At some point one of the other girls must have told me that was the hole where the baby came out. I rejected the idea. I had seen the collection of objects month by month, and I knew we were talking about something the size of a melon. There was no way that was coming out of there. A girl called Carol claimed she put two fingers in together when she was in the bath, but everyone else agreed it was the right size for one.

I wondered if there was some kind of special trick, where the baby slid out the size of a tadpole then puffed up as soon as it hit the air. In that case, was there a danger the baby might slip out at any moment, when you were on the toilet, and you had to catch it? What if you were not brave enough to put your hand into the toilet water and fish it out? But why would it grow so big inside first, and then shrink to get out? It was very confusing. I asked Lindsey about it. She lifted up her stretchy yellow jumper and showed me her spectacular caesarean scar.

'Too bloody right they're too big to get out,' she said. 'Anne-Marie was only six pounds and this is where they lifted her out. Best way.' She held my hand and ran it all along the jagged edge of scar tissue, from her belly button to the top of her lacy pants.

That must have been the year I turned ten, when Lindsey stopped looking after us because she had Anne-Marie, who I thought was named after me, but Edward said it was a totally different name.

After that her sister Melanie came to look after us, but Lindsey usually came round anyway to keep her company and to get out from under her mother's feet. She used to say, 'I've brought Anne-Marie to play with Joe,' but Anne-Marie was far too little to play. The most fun thing she could do was blow bubbles.

That was when I heard about the telephone box baby. It was on the radio. Someone had found a baby in a telephone box. Now this seemed like a far more sensible solution than either the tiny hole or the big sharp knife.

I hoped the baby in the telephone box was wrapped up well enough. There was a telephone box in our village but it had quite a few windows missing. I had been in it myself, and it smelled of wee. There was a directory chained to the little black shelf. I didn't think it was a safe place to leave a baby. I remembered how careful you had to be about germs. Also, what if the baby was left in the telephone box and no one found it for a day? It would freeze to death or starve. Or both.

I regularly walked past the telephone box on my way home from school. Lindsey and Melanie would be walking with me, one pushing Joe in his little stripy pushchair, one with Anne-Marie in her huge pink throne. They didn't mind my running on ahead and checking the telephone box. They would call out, 'Don't touch anything in there. It's all dirty!' and I pretended I had some stupid game about phoning someone up.

I never told anyone I was checking for the baby. I was worried the baby would be smelly to start with, from being in that horrible place, yellow-skinned like the old paper inside the directory. Perhaps he would be wrapped up in newspaper or in pages torn from the telephone book. He would have no name, no home, no one. I would take him home and keep him. I didn't care where other people got their babies from. All their ideas were disgusting. This one was mine, and I knew where I was going to find him.

I thought about how hard it would be to carry him home. I knew babies wriggled like crazy, and this one would have no clothes, so he would be slippery. It's at least a mile and a half from the telephone box out past the church around to the next junction by the river and along to our house. Would I manage to hold on to him the whole way? Would I remember the right way to carry him? Would he cry? Would he get cold?

I imagined getting him home, and setting up the baby bath on the floor, the way we used to with Joe, lifting him out gently with a warm towel, finding him one of Joe's old Babygros in the back of the airing cupboard, warming up a bottle of milk. But in all the time I carried this fantasy – and I never walked past the telephone box without checking for him – I never imagined past those first few hours. Did I really think I would be allowed to keep him?

I told people about it, when I was old enough for it to be a joke. And one day, when I was in my twenties, I got a message from a friend: Hey, someone found your baby in the telephone box – check it out. She had sent me a link to a local newspaper. Not in my home village, but one very like it, somewhere in Lincolnshire. A baby in a telephone box. Freezing cold, wrapped in newspaper, exactly as I had imagined. So lucky someone heard him cry before it was too late. His young mother had been found already.

But before the grown-up brain kicked in, and registered the fear and pain of the young girl who left him there, the danger to both their lives, I felt robbed. That was my first impulse. My baby had finally been found, and not by me. After the loss, the second thought, second heartbeat, guilt. Why had I stopped looking? How could I have been so disloyal?

I didn't find Susannah in a telephone box. But I did look for her in some unlikely places before I found her. I looked for her in relationships with people who had no interest in me, let alone any child I might conceive. I looked for her in one-night stands. I looked for her on the pages of adoption agencies who would never consider an application from a single young woman without full-time employment. I persuaded a friend at university to provide a film canister of donated sperm once a month in return for a round of drinks and an agreement handwritten on the back of one of his art history essays that I would never ask for any child maintenance payments.

The trouble was that his hall of residence was a bus ride from mine, and he said it was too disgusting to let me administer it in his bathroom, so I had to carry it home tucked inside my shirt and hope it didn't go cold. It probably went cold. In any case it never worked. He did suggest we try a more direct route, any time I felt like it. But I said no. Not because I didn't like him, but because I was afraid I would like him too much. Pure gratitude had already made me like him too much.

All through my twenties I looked for her in a series of bad decisions and dead ends. But in the end I found myself pregnant with Susannah in a far more conventional way. I fell in love. It turns out all those clichés and bad pop songs were right. Not believing in it, not thinking it applied to me, none of that protected me. I was working in a gallery. There was one of his paintings that I really liked, a stack of different-coloured shoes and boots. One day he was standing in front of it. He asked what I thought of it. I said it was my favourite, because of the colours.

'Good job you said that. It's mine.'

'Well, you seem to own a lot of very nice shoes.'

He turned around from the painting then and smiled at me. I was suddenly aware of the precise distance between us, not only the distance between his voice and mine, a space of live air I could measure with my breath, but the distance between our bodies, our legs, all the way to the space between his feet and mine. I looked down, to duck out of the eye contact. He was wearing bright blue Doc Marten boots. Mine were dark red.

'Good boots.'

We both looked up at the same time. And I knew that I would believe everything he said. Every word. As he took a half-step back away from me, and said, 'Right, well. See you again I s'pose. If you take any more of my pictures.' He shrugged and left. I could feel the tug of empty air as he walked away, and found myself following him to the door, holding it open behind him, watching him walk away.

At the corner he took a striped woolly hat out of his coat pocket and pulled it on. He had a boyish walk, a sort of bouncing, dancing way of walking. I thought of the word 'jaunty'. A jaunty hat. A jaunty walk. Jaunty is not a sexy word. I laughed out loud, and he heard and turned to wave.

I spent the next week reading his file and learning everything in it, and trying to persuade the gallery owner to buy more of his paintings. No one wanted to buy the pile of shoes, and the gallery owner was only there once every few weeks, so I hadn't made any progress when he came back to talk to me. He was waiting on the doorstep when I came to open up.

What he said was something like, 'You didn't sell my shoes then?' and what I said was something like, 'What are you doing here?' He didn't even pretend he was there to see Donald, the owner, or that he was bringing any work to sell.

He said, 'I came to see you. I thought we could go out to dinner, or something. Get to know each other.' I couldn't even reply. I just stared at him. 'You know my name already, off the painting. I'm Barney. And you are?'

'Marianne.'

'Very romantic. Of the moated grange.'

'Well, it was more like a bog really. A boggy track. A track that flooded. You can call it a moat if you like.'

'How do you feel about posing?'

'What?'

'For a portrait. Is that your natural hair colour, or did something go wrong with the dye?'

'It was supposed to come out blonde. Blondish.'

'Maybe you could wear a hat?'

'A jaunty hat? Could be arranged.'

'Jaunty? Now that's not a word you hear every day, Marianne of the moated grange.'

It turned out he had a lot of hats in his studio. Hats with embroidered mirrors and straw trilbies, and crocheted bonnets. He drew me in a knitted skullcap. All through the drawing he never broke the glass between us. I was looking away from him. I couldn't tell how he was looking at me. It was only when I saw the finished drawing that I understood how well he had seen me.

Still we didn't cross the precisely measured space between us. Where I had countered my natural mistrust of everyone by sleeping with anyone but never attaching any importance to it, Barney's mistrust of everyone made him keep away. He was wary. Very wary. We spent a year meeting and talking about painting and never asking about anything else. His online profile was strictly about his work.

It was ten months before he told me he had a girlfriend. That didn't stop me calling him. Or lying in wait for him in cafés and galleries and anywhere else I could think of. I would bring something I'd been reading and offer to swap. He even tried to read *Pearl*. No one else has ever offered to do that for me. I took it as a sign of profound interest. I suppose it might have been a sign of his profound interest in poetry rather than in me. He recited some of it back to me, and ever since I've heard it in his voice. He grew up near the Green Chapel. The real one, not the one on the river near our house. So perhaps he really did sound like the Gawain poet.

One thing we disagreed about was my attachment to the memories of my mother. Why did I even care? He didn't get it. He didn't like me to talk about her. Even my saluting magpies and singing old songs annoyed him. Because he knew it was all about her. His own mother had disappeared when he was eight. But he never wanted to hear from her again. He knew she was alive, but he didn't want to see her. I kept asking questions about her. He told me she lived in Market Drayton with her second husband, and they ran a livery stable. I couldn't help imagining my own mother only an hour's drive away, her hair grey over the ears, still falling out of a twist on the back of her head, her eyes creased into wrinkles as she walked her horse gently on its leading rein into the sunlight of the livery yard. I looked up the bus routes and asked if we could go and see her. He looked as if I'd slapped him, swallowed hard and said, 'This is my mother we're talking about. She didn't want me when I was eight, and she won't want me now.' Then he left the room very quietly and sadly, and as the door closed I imagined the empty clothes hangers in the wardrobe echoing their thirty-year percussion track in the song of his loss.

He loved Edward and Joe. He seemed very comfortable in a house run by a man. Which makes perfect sense. The only one of us he mistrusted was me. He already thought all women were either mad or deeply untrustworthy, or both. He watched me carefully for any sign that would confirm his suspicions. All I had to do to hang on to him was to keep proving I was not like my mother. But unfortunately I am. And it's hard work hanging all your love on a peg that is trying to prove a point.

We had not been together long enough to talk openly about a future, a family, but right from the start that was what I wanted. I wanted the whole deal. I wanted it badly enough to wait for the right moment. And I thought he did too. He gave Edward a painting of an old shed in the woods, and hung it in his office. It's still there. He drew me a thousand times, usually when I was looking away. We talked about maybe moving in together one day, when my rental contract was up.

Then we got very drunk on free wine at the opening night of an exhibition of miniature prints, and we compounded the drunkenness with some horrible cheap pizzas on the way home, and I threw up so much I ought to have considered the pill null and void for the rest of the month. But I didn't really take the whole pill thing that seriously after the year of failed sperm donation.

A week or so later he went out with his friends to celebrate one of them winning first prize in the miniature print exhibition. He brought them all back to his flat, where I was staying that night for some reason, and I was a bit rude about being woken up, and a bit ruder still when they played music very loudly for two hours after that.

In the morning he told me that (a) I had embarrassed him the night before, behaving like I owned the place, which I absolutely did not, and nor would I ever, come to that, and (b) he and all his friends had made a pact that night never to have children in case they interfered with their art. I was too young and stupid to know when to back off, and to know that it's best not to argue with a man with a hangover. At some point in the argument I mentioned the pizza-induced puking and the pill, and he accused me of tricking him and hijacking his life without his consent.

By the time I did the first pregnancy test we were still walking around each other tentatively, our smiles in constant danger of falling into tears, and I didn't dare mention it right away. So when I did mention it, I had to admit I had kept it secret. Which made it all the more suspicious.

When I stayed at my flat all week to demonstrate I was not expecting him to invite me to live with him just because I was pregnant, he accused me of walking out on him now I'd got the only thing I wanted. Every time I cried he asked if it was real emotion or only hormones. By becoming a mother I had become untrustworthy, borderline crazy. Everything he feared.

We carried on tiptoeing around each other for the next

three months, at which point I started bleeding. He looked relieved. And I couldn't bear it. I couldn't bear how happy he looked. I went home to cry my way through the remaining months of intermittent bleeding and terror on my own. So I can't even blame him for leaving. It was me.

We might still have got back together just after Susannah was born, but unfortunately when he came to visit his week-old daughter I was insane. He arrived just as Susannah woke up for a feed, and I was too embarrassed to undo my shirt in front of him and reveal my broken bleeding nipples and mound of belly. What I wanted was to hand him the baby so I could go and have a shower and brush my hair, but now she was awake and hungry it was too late for that.

I handed Susannah to him, and he said, 'It's hard to see her face for the screaming.' He didn't like her name. Or at least I worried he didn't like her name. He hadn't said anything either way. I wondered if he was avoiding saying it.

I could feel the familiar awareness of his body, of the precise distance between us, the shape of the child clearly marked out as if I had drawn her there in red ink. Everything in the room started to leak colour. His face, his dark brown hair, his soft striped shirt, his black jeans and his woollen socks with red and orange toes started to bleach and buckle and the redness leaked into a pool around our feet.

I could smell the colour, its blood and cat fur and old coats in damp cupboards. I was afraid he would look down and see all our colour pooling into the carpet, that he would smell its bad smell and know there were cats in the house, with their germs and half-dead mice and their baby-smothering pelts.

We were both still standing in the middle of the room

looking at a screaming child with a name only one of us liked, when the midwife arrived. I could see her at the front door. It was not the friendly one, who had promised to bring me medicine for piles. It was the Scottish one who said 'germs' with a rolled 'r' to make them sound more scary.

I handed the baby to Barney and went to open the door, but I was moving my feet carefully, trying not to spread the colour around. I didn't want the floor to look dirty. In the tiny hallway I looked down and saw I was surrounded by cats. That made sense to me. I had smelled them, after all, and here they were.

Now I was worried about the germs that cats bring in. Also, Barney hates cats. If I opened the door for the scary midwife she would see the cats and realise I was making a bad job of looking after the baby. She was already concerned about my poor latching technique. I stood with my back to the door, trying to shoo the cats away from my feet.

The sound of Susannah crying was making the milk pour down inside my shirt. I could feel a puddle gathering on the soft waist of my jogging bottoms. I stared down at my feet, willing the cats to go away. I concentrated on the tile patterns on the floor. They were very nice tiles.

When I moved in Barney had bought a special tile-restoring cleaner and scrubbed them till the colours shone. Oranges and creams with tiny turquoise triangles. If I concentrated very hard on them I could see through the cats. Not totally. But the cats faded out. I began to think the cats were some kind of test. That maybe they weren't real cats. I knew you cannot see through real cats, not even sometimes.

Barney stepped into the hallway carrying Susannah.

'Shall I let her in? What can I do to help?'

'Get the cats out of here before she sees them!' I saw him blink, adjust, swallow hard. So I knew something was wrong. But he held eye contact.

'That sounds like a good idea. You come in here and feed this hungry baby, and I'll tell her to come back later.'

'Tell her to send the other one. The other one has medicine.' For some reason I was whispering the last word of every sentence. He settled me into the armchair and handed me Susannah. The wet patch had spread all through my sweatshirt. I saw him staring at it, perplexed. And when I looked up into his face he was bright orange. Not like he'd painted it. Not like a bad tan. Like he'd lit a bright orange light inside it. I reached my hand up to touch it, wondering if it was hot. But it wasn't.

'Marianne, sweetheart. I think you're a bit ill.'

'I think I might be.'

'I'm going to tell that woman to go away now. And call your dad.'

'And Barney?'

'Yeah?'

'You could ask her about your face. She's a kind of nurse.'

'My face?'

'You can't go round with an orange face forever!'

'No, right.'

When he came back in with a sandwich I was worried the cats might come back into the room with him, but they didn't. I could still smell them a bit from the hallway, though, and it occurred to me they must have eaten up all the red ink that was on the floor. I became quite interested in the floor. I looked under the sofa to see if the ink had gone under there.

'Will you be alright now?'

I wasn't sure what he meant. He was the one with the orange face. Unless it was catching.

'Make sure all the cats are gone. I can't have cats inside. It's insanitary.'

'I'll make sure they all go out the back door.'

'Right.'

Even as he told me that, I began to think these were not real cats. Like the way you realise when you are drunk that the pub carpet is not really moving up and down. Even though you keep tripping up on it when it does.

I heard him on his phone in the kitchen. I heard him through the sound of the kettle and the fridge opening and closing. Now he would be telling someone I was mad. And even if the sometimes see-through cats were all gone, they would see I let someone into the house with a probably catching orange face. And they would come and take the baby. I knew I had to run away, but she was feeding, and I was too tired for running and I would bleed too much to get very far.

Edward was there in thirty minutes, and stayed for three weeks, bringing me endless glasses of milk and making me my mother's best black-treacle flapjack and making sure I slept all night while he warmed up bottles of formula, putting on endless loads of laundry and keeping the constant medical visitors appeased and fed with cups of tea, until there were no cats, and no smells of cats, and no people looking in through the glass in the front door.

He stayed until my nipples had scabbed over and turned into tough little leather pockets with no feeling left in them and Susannah looked up at him and smiled her first smiles and loved him forever the way she would have loved her father, if he had been the one to be there and do all those things.

Nobody talked about taking Susannah away. That was Edward's gift to me. But it was also my mother's. Edward had spent all the years since my mother walked out of the door wishing he had known better and stayed with her after Joe was born until the angels stopped living on the stairs. There was no way he was leaving me alone for a minute.

I didn't see a lot of Barney after that first visit, though Edward tells me he phoned every week to ask how I was. Apparently he came over and walked Susannah in circles round the park in her pram some afternoons, but I don't remember that. I do remember the look on his face when he started to come and take her out for the day when she was eighteen months old. He looked embarrassed, as if he had been the one to go crazy. Embarrassed at seeing it, I suppose.

From time to time he brought things his sisters had handed on from their children, or home-made mobiles to hang over the cot. When Susannah was two he spent an afternoon taking photos of her, which turned out really well. He's not very good with birthdays or Christmases, but he turns up at other times with interesting surprises. A scooter that trails sparks. A hardly worn bright yellow duffel coat. A cookery book. A huge plastic tub of Lego he found in a charity shop, which turned out to have Sylvanian Families scattered through it like a lucky dip.

He still can't look me in the eye, but he does love his daughter. He lives in France now, but he keeps in touch with her. If he had any money he would probably send that too. It hurts me to see how much he loves her. How easily she fits under his arm, how they like the same music, laugh at the same things. How easily those same things could have added up to a far better life for us all.

But they didn't. And now they never will. Because Susannah became the way he learned not to lose a daughter. When his next one came along with a different mother, he knew to stick around and ignore the temporary hormone-soup-strangeness.

In a weird kind of way I was right all along. I was looking for the most unlikely stroke of luck. A chance in a million a baby would be left in a telephone box only minutes before I walked by. That I would be the one to find her. That she would still be warm, and safe. A lottery ticket of a chance every time. In my case, all my good fortune rolled up into one throw of the dice. The perfect six. My beautiful daughter. Everyone expected me to name her after my mother, but I didn't want it to be too obvious, so I named her Susannah Pearl.

17

The Exit Sign

Here comes a candle
To light you to bed
And here comes a chopper
To chop off your head.

Last year my landlord decided to upgrade all his houses on this road, so we all got new plastic windows and new fuse boxes followed by a steep rise in rent. The new fuse box is very sensitive. It doesn't like the washing machine much. It can detect any moisture under the kettle, and you can't use the toaster and kettle at the same time. It trips off so frequently I've had to hang a little torch on the inside of the understairs cupboard to see my way in to flip it back. When I mentioned it to the landlord he said, 'So it's working, yes? I did all that to keep you safe, you see.' Nothing to do with the electric work being done by one of his dodgy cousins.

I have a pretty sensitive trip switch too. It can flip over

from reality to invention in a heartbeat. One time the dentist used novocaine on me I thought my legs had grown too big for the room and were sticking out into the street. I am assuming this is genetic. I guess my mother had a similar problem. Common causes for the trip switch to cut out are sleep loss, high temperature, fear, shock, jump scares, stress. Sleep loss is number one. And that February my mother had a new baby. You don't get better sleep loss than that.

Every human has a trip switch. Built into everyone's brain is the point at which the information from the senses becomes totally unreliable. What we see and hear and smell and taste bears no relation to what is actually there. So the brain goes into overdrive, making up more and more ludicrous explanations for the strange information coming in on all sides.

I feel slightly less guilty about my trip switch now I know we all have one. Even though it turns out mine is not a very good one. But it's not the worst electrical circuit in my head. I can live with the trip switch. The one I have trouble with is the exit sign.

You'd think I'd be the last person on earth to look for a quick exit, knowing what it's like to be left behind. But I'm in a high-risk category. When someone close to us steps into that river and never comes out of it, the rest of us are left with the possibility. It lights up an exit sign in our heads, like the ones over a fire door at the end of a hotel corridor, through this set of doors, then the next, the sign is lit up all day and all night, even if the emergency generator has to kick in.

And once that sign has been lit in our heads, it is very difficult to switch it off. I have argued with the sign. I have chosen to ignore it. I have pushed open one of those stubborn fire doors, and seen the way lit up for my feet, the string of tiny blue lights along the edge of the corridor, and deliberately turned myself around and tried to find my way back to where I belong. Sometimes it has felt to me as if all the other pathways are more difficult, more twisted and indistinct. Sometimes it has felt as if the only path is the one lit up for me by that sign.

I have learned to turn away from it, with enormous effort, to feel my way back into the darkness where I belong, listening intently for clues that will take me back towards safety. When I had Susannah I made a pact with that exit sign, to turn my face away from it as often as it appeared, and move into the relative safety of a place where I could see her, hear her, pick her up. Even then, I couldn't switch it off. I could only make a deal with it.

The exit sign has something to do with my never finishing anything. Like writing this down. I don't know how many times I have written this, how many versions there are, all of them unfinished, on obsolete files, floppy discs, in paper folders where the staples have become crusted and orange. If I say there are at least three versions that don't have Susannah in them, and she is a teenager now, you'll get some idea of the scale of it.

I would go back for the Wakes, and take the dog along the river path, and collect the rushes, and see the building work on the old house, admire the espaliered orchard, and I'd think, I must finish writing down all that stuff. Then that dog died, and I had Susannah, and got another dog, and I would be carrying her in a sort of baby backpack or holding her by the hand, and the dog would be jumping about on the edge of the river and I would still be thinking, where did I leave that last attempt, did I ever find a way to finish it?

And I would go home and forget about it and remember about it, and feel bad about both. Was it more disloyal to finish it, as if any version could fully contain my extraordinary mother, and all that she meant to me, or to leave it half-finished, as if I didn't care?

At first I said it was for Joe. That made it sound like a noble task, to leave an account of his mother, because he could not remember her or the place where he was born. But that ended up feeling like cruelty. All I could do was list all the things he had missed, and all the ways in which our way of life after she left was a kind of betrayal.

He has a few photographs Edward and I picked out for him, so he knows what his mother looked like. More or less. She hated having her photograph taken.

In one of them she is in the garden, sitting under a tree. You can't see much of her, and the shade from the tree falls across her face. The other one is of her and Joe and me on the sofa not long after Joe is born. She is looking at me and laughing, we are nose to nose, the same nose, same chin, same tangled hair. Joe looks like a red blob in a white Babygro. I wonder what we were laughing at. I have no memory of the photograph being taken. I don't even recognise the sofa.

I made an agreement with myself never to do the same as my mother until I had recorded faithfully everything I remember about her. I made this deal before Susannah was born, and I then had to add a codicil, that I would wait until my child was at least eighteen before I walked out and never came back.

I thought eighteen would be old enough. Never having had a mother past the age of eight, I reasoned that eighteen would be plenty. But then I noticed that I missed my mother more than ever when I had a child of my own, and had to rethink. Perhaps Susannah might prefer me to be around when she has a child? Perhaps there would still be work to do.

So all the unfinished handwritten versions I tried to say were for Joe went into the attic to be eaten by mice. Then I moved on to word processors, and discovered a whole new set of ways to lose everything I wrote. Cheap laptops are the perfect co-conspirator for the self-eliminator.

And if I get to the end of it this time, does it mean I have to make a whole new bargain with the exit sign? Or will the devil be waiting for me when I get to the last page, arms folded across his chest, a knowing smile? Got you, at last. You've written your farewell note. It's taken you long enough. Over thirty years you've been putting off the moment when you look up from your cutting-out on the kitchen table, and realise something is wrong, and run out of the back door along the river path after your mother.

Now you've finally run out of excuses. Hand in your written paper and leave the exam hall. We gave you extra time, but now they are turning off the lights and folding away the little desks, and there is only one door left open. It's marked exit.

I have blamed my mother for handing on the exit sign, for making me feel unworthy of my life. I felt ashamed that I was not enough to keep her here, that she could turn away from my voice, and Edward's, and Joe's. But that was before I knew about Jonathan. How could I have made a deal with that sign, if the voice of my child was on the other side of it? I don't think I could.

If you are a mother you are always to blame. I know that now. If you did not give birth to them too slowly or too quickly, underfeed them, overfeed them, pick them up, set them down, push them forward, hold them back, love them too little or too much, you are to blame for their very existence. You loaded them with your own dodgy genetic package and sent them out into the world to deal with its particular set of time bombs.

And then there are the environmental factors. Poverty is a risk factor. For all kinds of illness. And Susannah did know about that. She knew about the letters for school trips when we ticked the box to ask for a reduction in the cost. She knew her dinner money did not come in an envelope from home, but was added on to the account by the secretary. Her uniform came from the second-hand bench in the sports hall. Her shoes did not have secret keys under them and little dolls in the heels like the rich girls had. None of that ever seemed to matter. It never crossed my mind it could make her ill.

Moving house is a risk factor. If you rent on twelve-month contracts it is a fact of life. From the age of five to eight Susannah never lived anywhere long enough for it to be worth putting up pictures. I didn't like it much, but I didn't mind much either. Susannah always protested for the week it took to pack up and move on, but in between she never mentioned it. But it doesn't matter whether or not she said so. The fact remains it is on the list of risk factors for mental illness.

Single parenting is also a risk factor. Apparently it makes them anxious. The children take on too adult a role. They feel responsible for the one parent they have. They feel less secure. And I am to blame in this. I never encouraged her to see her other parent as a viable alternative, a safe back-up plan. I never encouraged her to see him at all.

Feeling to blame for someone's illness does not help you to keep your temper or keep your patience with the medics or stop you from crying when you are in a queue to talk to your bank about your medium-to-long-term borrowing requirements and your phone runs out of credit. Feeling to blame makes you snappy and irritable and inadequate and defeated. None of those is on the list of desirable attributes in a parent.

Parents are supposed to be organised and good at getting out of bed, reliable as to days of the week, after-school clubs, and direct debit payments. They wear sensible shoes. They always have a snack in their bag. Parents remember to write your name in your school wellies in indelible ink. They bring back the permission slip in time for next term's violin lessons. They don't drop you off at school an hour late with a banana in your pocket for breakfast.

Parents are stuck in a 1950s reading book, where they come complete with a full set of matching grandparents who smoke pipes and grow flowers and read bedtime stories. Had I considered the impact on my own child of having a missing-probably-dead grandmother? Had I stopped to think for a minute that the fracture in my family, the rift that opened in my own heart, would be passed down to the next generation, through my own damage if nothing else?

No, I hadn't. It never crossed my mind. I thought my child would heal my broken heart. I didn't stop to ask if this was asking too much of her. I didn't stop to think about what was passed on in my milk, the hurt, the loss, the anxiety. I remember feeding her, looking around for my own mother, crying as I hadn't for years, the tears falling on my baby's head, and I never thought those tears would leave a trace. I thought they would disappear as easily as I brushed them away with my hand.

There's an exercise the therapists make you do. Where you are allowed to blame everyone. I have played that game, or tried to. Who do I blame for my mother's disappearance? My mother, first off. My father, for not knowing she might. For being at work. Mrs Wynne, for not seeing her set off. Myself, for looking at some cut-out dolls instead of watching her every move. Joe, for staying asleep all afternoon. Her midwife, for not fighting her way down our muddy lane to fill in the questionnaire to assess post-natal depression risk. If such a thing existed at the time. The GP she had seen three days before to weigh Joe, who noticed nothing out of the ordinary. My brother Jonathan, for not drawing breath.

But none of them is to blame. I am not even sure what is the point of the blame exercise. I didn't like playing it. Who does it help? What if no one is to blame? I prefer the word accident. Or the official one. Misadventure. Death by misadventure. Because I like the word adventure. That describes her well. My mother's life was an adventure. But it went wrong.

18

Art Therapy

Up the ladder and down the wall
A penny loaf will serve us all.

You find milk, and I'll find flour
And we'll have pudding in half an hour.

Edward and I both find it hard to take credit for anything good. We failed to keep her alive, so what does it matter what kind of degree I got, or if he was made head of department? But those things do matter. It took me a long time to work out that they do. And I am still trying to work out how to live with that realisation, how to balance my love of my work with a sense of my unworthiness to do it.

What I do is a thing called art therapy, which means setting up semicircles of easels in community centres and encouraging people to become absorbed and engaged in something outside their own distress for half a day and then take something away at the end.

It pays thirty pounds an hour, excluding travel and expenses, and during term time it keeps us very nicely. In the school holidays I work at the café at the end of our road, and Susannah spends a lot of time with Edward. This pays minimum wage and the owner keeps the tips, but I get a free lunch and take home leftover bread and occasional jars of things that are out of date.

In both places I have to be unnaturally cheerful and upbeat; I listen to a lot of sad stories and watch people carefully for any signs they are about to become upset. In both places I spend more time clearing up after people than I spend with them face to face, and in both places a lot of the clearing up happens after the hours I am paid for.

I hear just as many tales of misery and loneliness in the café as I do in the Age UK-sponsored classes. I have heard of long prison sentences dealt out for random, momentary acts of unintentional harm, custody battles so costly that they leave the parent homeless, lonely old people who order their prescriptions to arrive on separate days just so there's an excuse to queue up at the pharmacy where someone will greet them and say their name, others who set their alarm to meet the milk delivery on their doorstep, just to say hello.

My favourite place to work is the mental health day-care centre in the middle of an allotment. Or it was, until last year. Susannah was running a temperature till the early hours, so I couldn't send her to school. I slept through my alarm, and by the time I called Edward to see if he could come and babysit he had already left for work. Who else could I ask?

If I'd had any sense I would have called in sick right away, but I was still hoping I could go, somehow, and I started to imagine my students already setting off in their special taxis, or taking the long way round the town centre because they were afraid of crowds, or pushing their sad old shopping trolleys onto buses where no one wants to sit next to them because they look odd, and they smell of the damp bedsit where they are waiting for supported housing to be approved.

So I called Carrie. I like Carrie. She lives further down our road, and she rents from the same landlord because he is the only one for miles who will take single parents who don't have full-time employment, and also pets. Carrie has four boys and three dogs. Her house is noisy and smells of dogs and her oldest son's weed habit, but when she steps out of it she smells like new clothes, like pear drops and green hair gel. She listens to local radio all day, and believes an astonishing range of conspiracy theories she finds on Facebook. But she is also brave, and loving, and fiercely proud of all her boys.

She keeps saying she still wants a girl, she's going to keep on trying till she gets one. Every time she comes round she wants to paint Susannah's nails or plait her hair, but Susannah won't go along with it. She can't stand her. I think Carrie's boys are so often in trouble at school that Susannah's afraid the teachers will associate her with them, that the boys might call out her name in the yard or show they know her from somewhere.

Most of all she hates that we have things in common, Carrie and I. That I am happy to acknowledge what we have in common, to share a cigarette in her backyard or make her cups of sweet tea all evening while she waits for the oldest to be sent back from the police station. It's not just things in common, or expediency, either. I like Carrie. I admire her early-morning face of perfect make-up, her brave vest tops and determined skinny jeans, the astonishing muscles in her arms that mean she can bring home the box of tinned goods from Home Bargains and not waste the 20p discount prices on a bus fare.

One Saturday when Carrie and I got drunk downstairs and her boys played music too loud further down the street, Susannah came downstairs to announce, 'When I grow up I'm going to have a real family, with two parents, and everyone living together.' Carrie burst out laughing and sprayed white wine all over Susannah's favourite cat-design cushion. I said, 'Well, good luck with that. Yeah, why not?' before I collapsed in drunken giggles. Susannah took her cat cushion off to the kitchen to sponge it down, and stalked back upstairs to put it to dry in the airing cupboard.

For all her belief in Facebook news and cheap horoscopes, Carrie is sharp. When I brought her a jar of our damson jam made from free hedgerow pickings, she said it tasted bitter, and pointed out I'd spent more on the sugar than value jam at 22p a jar, not to mention the petrol to drive out to collect fruit and the cost of cooking. When I said it was fun picking fruit and making jam she laughed and said, 'That's like fun for OLD people, Maz!' She thinks a lot of my fun is for old people, like making yogurt and patchwork blankets.

But despite her sharpness, she's kind-hearted. All three of her horrible snarling heavy-jawed dogs came from lives in chains, one in a pub cellar, one under the railway bridge, one she found locked in the backyard tied up with washing line when she moved in.

I chickened out of waking Susannah to tell her who was babysitting for the day. I let myself set off, pretending it was better to let her sleep. Quoting to myself the consultant who said I needed to be watchful of any sleep loss. To call the helpline if she wasn't sleeping. So Carrie was setting up her nail polish in the kitchen, retuning the radio to Heart FM, flicking through yesterday's *Guardian* in search of her horoscope, when I woke Susannah by accident when I wheeled my bike along the hallway and banged it against the front door.

She appeared like a vengeful wraith on the landing, feverish in her white nightgown, hair spiralling out of her overnight plaits lit like copper in the landing light, a stream of vitriol and viral particles falling into the stairwell and evaporating over my head.

I was going anyway by then. It was too late to call in sick, and besides, I wanted to get out of there. I wanted to cycle as fast as I could down the diesel stink of the bus lane over the pedestrian bridge and out the other side of town to the allotments where the day-care centre had been built out of donated oddments of other buildings. If I rode fast enough I would blow away everything she said. Except I couldn't.

Every child knows the form of words that will create a shortcircuit into parental fury. The one that works on me is 'Why can't you be a normal mother?' In this case, 'Why can't you stay at home when I'm ill, like a normal mother?' It shoots adrenaline round my system. It blinds me with fury. It sent my pedals flying all the way to work so fast I made up the lost time and arrived for the start-of-day meeting, in time to smile at everyone and say, 'Today we are painting a garden. It's based on photographs of the allotment. We'll be mixing up lots of different greens.' And to hold up my version and count how many opted in, and set up the easels they needed, and an extra one for Janine, who is always late.

And then some of the other things she said found a way back into my mind past the screen of anger. Things like 'Have you even asked me how I'm feeling?' and 'Poor you, your daughter is too crazy to go to school, even if she says she's fine, poor you, because you're not the crazy one, are you? With your stupid secret diets that everyone knows are not secret? And your covered-up arms?'

Some of the students had gone into the kitchen to start making lunch for everyone, and the tables were stacked away to make space for the morning's painting class, the paints dished out in little blobs around old dinner plates, the canvases with helpful outlines arranged on the easels. I had added a brick wall in the background, and a brightly painted door. Near the front was an optional curved bench. I handed out traced patterns for cats on the bench, or under it, if they chose.

Most of the students had settled down to work. Only Big Sheila was wandering from easel to easel still, saying, 'Fuck me that's fucking gorgeous that is,' and putting a pebble into the swear box each time. The very quiet vicar's wife was – as usual – putting colourful blotches over all my guidelines in silent rebellion.

Then I started to show them how to use the outline of the gate in the far wall, to show an open door, if they wanted, rather than a closed one. I remembered Susannah saying, 'Just go then, but don't be surprised if I'm not here when you get back. Just don't expect me to be where you left me.' I drew the two simple lines inside the rectangle of the gate, the shadow of the opening along one edge, and I saw Susannah lift the catch on the long-gone gate at the end of our old garden, unwind the piece of orange twine we used to hold it shut, and slip out onto the river path. I saw the flash of her red coat as she moved out of my picture, heard her giggle, the sound of the river gathering speed behind her.

I started to shake and feel sick. I didn't know where I was, only that I had to get away, find her then and there before it was too late. Apparently I shouted and cried. I don't remember that bit. And I was calling her Margaret, my mother's name, which is weird, because I only ever called her Mummy.

Everyone there knew how to recognise a panic attack, and they were totally unfazed, sorting out a taxi to get me home, where Susannah had accepted Calpol and sweet tea from Carrie and was submitting to having her nails done at the kitchen table wrapped in my dressing gown with the dog asleep on her feet. I went back the next day to collect my bike and my paints.

They suspended me. They were nice, but they needed an art therapist, not another patient. Some of the students had been upset. They let me take a bag of donated food home with me, because I cried and said something dramatic like, 'What will become of us?'

What became of us was that Edward helped to pay our rent until some extra shifts came up at the café, and the day-care centre had gone through all the rounds of interviews with risk assessment officers they needed for me to go back to work. It took about nine months.

That was when I began to think about Edward's career. How had he managed to keep his job when I was refusing to go to school? How had he managed all those appointments with the Adolescent Mental Health Unit? And all of Joe's visits to the eczema specialist in Liverpool? How had he done it?

I looked back on those dinners of slightly burnt fish fingers in a sliced bread sandwich and an orange for pudding, and thought, well done. Protein, carbs and vitamin C. So what if we had the same thing the next day? I thought of him sitting in his car while Joe did football training, marking student work and piling it into the huge cardboard box on the passenger seat. Or sitting in the chlorine fog of a viewing gallery while I learned to swim, reading through a pile of student applications then pretending he really had seen me dive down and get that black brick from the bottom.

Back when hardly any fathers did any looking after at all, mine was taking me to endless appointments and monitoring my every meal, while holding on to his career and taking care of my little brother. I really ought to have been a more useful babysitter myself. I was old enough to help out in any number of ways. But I was pretty much useless all the way through to about seventeen.

I don't remember him complaining about it. The most I was aware of it was him standing in the doorway to some waiting room trying to call his department to rearrange something he was going to miss because my therapist was running late.

The nearest he came to mentioning it was when he said, 'Do what you can to hang on to your own work. It will keep you sane, in the end.' In the end. Meaning, sometime past the point where you are too brain-scrambled to know what you are doing. In the end. You'll be glad you kept your work.

With all those adoring students and young women joining his department over the years you might think he had a string of step-parenting females to take up the slack, but no. If he did have girlfriends, we never met them. And it's hard to see when he would have had the freedom or the time. Most single parents get weekends off when they can meet up with other partners or go out on dates. But that all depends on there being another parent out there somewhere, waiting their turn.

I don't think Joe is ever going to leave home, so it's not exactly ideal for bringing home women even now. Joe brings home plenty of friends of both sexes, and it's difficult to tell which are girlfriends and which are simply girls he knows. Joe didn't even leave home for university. He went to the one closest to home to save money, he says. And because he couldn't bear to leave behind his collection of crappy old motorbikes.

And with the two of them there living like eccentric bachelors with their weekly menus taped to the kitchen cupboards and their strange routines for cleaning everything on a fortnightly rota based on a points system no one except them can work out, it's pretty much like a student house anyway.

Joe has inherited Great-Uncle Matthew's talent for engineering design, and has more or less taken over the entire garden with a series of sheds tacked on to the brick garage, one leaning against the other. He has sheds for his push bikes and his surf board, for spare parts, and one plastic one with MISC painted on the side. His degree is in Intermediate Technology, a thing hardly anyone knows exists, which is basically making stuff work in places where your energy supply and machinery are either non-existent or very unreliable.

He has rigged up a static bicycle on the landing so that if you want to power the shower without switching on the electricity, someone can sit outside the room pedalling. Not that it is ever used. It was a project of some kind and neither of them feels like taking it down. He has at least three different kinds of solar panel on the roof of the garage. That cabin bed he slept in till he was thirteen is now an elaborate raised bed for growing vegetables watered by a system fed from the clean bathroom outlet. It pretty much blocks all the light to the kitchen window.

He keeps chickens in the front garden, which is now a slimy green mud patch. The chickens are not exactly free range but they think they are, and wander through all the nice neat gardens along the road. The cruelty of this is that Joe would have loved the Old House. Edward sometimes says, when he sees him carrying home a pair of escaped chickens, one under each arm, 'He's his mother's son.'

He's talking about my mother's chickens. Obliquely. Because it is one of the things we can't talk about any other way. She usually had six chickens, little black bantams with red feathery topknots and black feathery feet, who laid small, speckled eggs. The chickens came and went, but when new ones came along they always had the same names.

The first three were Elsie, Lacey and Tilly for the three sisters who lived in a Treacle Well in *Alice*, and then we got Elsie Two, Lacey Two and Tilly Two, because the next three chickens might be jealous the first ones got the best names.

They lived a long time under my mother's care. She rounded them up each twilight before the foxes were out, and counted them in by name before she locked them up for the night. She saved them scraps of food. I was never forced to eat things I didn't like. What was left on my plate went into the chicken bowl.

Whenever she walked out into the garden they would run after her, hoping for a little treat from the corn she kept in her coat pocket: she walked about the garden followed by a curved shadow of bantams sweeping around her like the train of a long feathery dress.

They didn't survive her long. A week, maybe two. I expect that old fox had been watching them for years, waiting for his chance. Several times we lost track of the afternoon and raced out just too late to try to find them before nightfall and had to lift them down from where they were nesting in the trees. One night we were late to put them to bed, and when Joe finally fell asleep so Edward and I could go out with a torch to find them, they were all dead.

We saw the first one on the path by the outhouse, only a few steps from the back door, and I thought it was a dead crow because her head was gone, and without her red feathery headdress she was all black. The next one was further up the path, sticking out of a patch of honesty, the feathers ragged and splayed so it looked like she had black socks full of holes half pulled off her sad yellow feet. Her neck was broken and her head was hanging off on a gory little string.

Edward said, 'Go inside, Marianne, this is not going to get any better.' But I kept on following him as he worked his way to the chicken house past another two corpses, to find the last two mangled and strewn across the blood-spattered nesting boxes.

We dug a grave for them under an apple tree, and it took a lot of digging. You need a really big hole and after a while the tree roots got in our way. We had to hang the torch from a branch to see what we were doing. The first time we tried to fit them into the hole they came right up to the surface.

Edward said, 'It's no good, we'll have to get them all out again and go deeper.' Neither of us said anything about it, except to comment on the size of hole we needed. From time to time he sent me back to the house to listen and make sure Joe was still asleep.

I did as much of the digging as I could, and we both gave ourselves horrific blisters. I wondered if he was thinking the same as I was when we first found them: how will we tell her when she comes home? And later, deep into the digging, the worst, the most evil thought: if she doesn't come back, she'll never know what we did.

It was about fourteen years later when Joe hatched out a bunch of chicks at secondary school in an incubator and brought them home in a cardboard box. I asked Joe what they were called.

'Bock,' he said. 'They're all called Bock. I asked them what name they wanted, and they all said the same.'

Edward asked what he intended to keep them in, and he said, 'Well, they are too young to go outside just yet. So I'll keep them in this box in the kitchen while I make a chicken house out of some stuff I found in a skip.' He has always found some stuff in a skip.

This stuff turned out to be a brown 1950s sideboard on fat knobbly legs. He screwed a metal bottom on it against foxes, painted it with waterproofing and tacked on felt for a roof. It did pretty well for about a year until he found some better stuff in a different skip, and upgraded them.

Once when Edward and I were watching Joe put a little windmill on the peak of the garage roof, Edward said, 'If we'd left him in the country, do you suppose he would have rebelled and done nothing but play with computers?' Edward doesn't say these things sadly. He cannot look at Joe and say things sadly. He looks at Joe as if rays of light were flying out of him. And perhaps they are.

19

A Pair of Iron Shoes

I went to my father's garden
To find an Irish farthing.

I gave it to my mother
To buy a baby brother.

My brother was so nasty
I baked him in a pasty.

The pasty wasn't tasty
So I threw it over the garden wall.

I threw it over the garden wall.
Die once! Die twice! Die three times
And never no more.

I used to have fantasies about our return to the Old House. How one day the new owners would wake up and realise they had not signed all the paperwork, and there was a secret clause in Great-Uncle Matthew's will that meant they were not allowed to live there, or lightning would strike the chimney in protest every time they drew up outside until they got the message and ran away.

Or one day they drove home from work and the whole house had lifted up gently on a huge brown sluggish flood and floated past them, the curtains at the windows waving goodbye as it set off of its own accord to find its true owners. Childish fantasies that I was too old to believe even at the time.

In all the years the old house was for sale and no one bought it there were long adult conversations about interest rates and shared access and a thing called a chain. Someone was always asking, are they in a chain? I was pretty vague as to what kind of chain that might be, and how they got themselves into it, but as any child can tell you, being in a chain is a bad thing.

The people who bought it in the end were chain-free. I was glad. I didn't want anyone dragging their shackles around on those cold stone floors, tragically clanking up the wooden stairs and dragging the metallic taste of sadness all over the ramshackle garden. It was muddy enough anyway.

I didn't meet the new owners. Edward invited me to come and show them around, after they had offered the money and wanted one more visit. He said I might find it easier to imagine them there if I had met them. I didn't want to imagine anyone there. If I had to imagine it at all I preferred my own inventions: melodramatic villains with thin moustaches and sinister women in long dresses sliding along the landing a few inches off the ground. Vicious ghosts. Crockery flying from the hands of a poltergeist. The slam of doors when no one was there to slam them. Faceless shadows with long dresses made of those sticky bombs of thistle heads we used to throw at each other in primary school.

But this time I went back to the house. Not inside it, or not inside any part of it that existed when I was a child. It was Sunday evening at the end of the Wakes, the fairground packing up and the smell of popcorn and diesel hanging on the hedges around the church.

Susannah had found a group of young teenagers from the village who had all been promised cheap rides on the thing called Flying Saucers if they stayed at the end of the day. I left her sitting on the edge of a group of girls in the triangle of shade behind the hot dog truck, all of them pulling up bits of grass and turning their bracelets round and round on their wrists. I said I wouldn't be long, but she was being too cool to reply, so I set off with the dog along the river to the Green Chapel to leave my customary bunch of flowers.

Quite near where our old gate used to lead onto the river path someone had made a new gate, a little white wooden one with a roof over it. It was nearly in the right place. But not quite. On the other side of the gate was a curved gravel path with wooden edges, borders filled with alliums and hollyhocks and all sorts of soft leafy plants.

Under the hedge and poking cheekily through the gravel in places was my mother's mint. Mint that ought to have been planted in a container, but she didn't know that, mint that has spread and multiplied and dodged and woven its way into every hedgerow and every border ever since.

Beyond the curved path was the softly orange brick wall of the vegetable garden, now covered very neatly in trellises and espaliered apple trees. I could see the wooden door in the garden wall half-open at the far end, painted a bright green. My dog was curious too, pulling at the lead and trying to stick his nose into some smell under the hedge.

There was someone pushing a wheelbarrow along the river path, only a few steps behind me, so I stepped inside the gate to let him pass. But he didn't. He stopped wheeling the barrow and said, 'Sorry, I'm heading in there. You'll need to step out this way.'

Which was how I met the new owner. By blocking the way back into his own garden. By the time we had swapped places and untangled the dog lead from the wheelbarrow and I had admired his new gate and the splendid alliums along his path and stopped the dog licking the muck off his wellies he had found out who I was. Joe's sister, he said.

In one way this was no surprise. Joe has friends wherever he goes. As soon as he went to school I became 'Joe's sister'. Quite often the kitchen at the New House is full of people who call me 'Joe's sister'. But in another way, it was wholly surprising. If I had never met the new owners, how had Joe managed it? Had he been visiting the place all his life, staying friends with these people, while the rest of us were locked out forever? Had we all been welcome here all along, and I was the only one stubborn enough to ignore it?

'I suppose you were here for the Wakes? Antonia's in the garden. Come round and meet her. Joe's sister! She'll be so pleased!'

I followed him round the corner of the walled garden and along the side of the old kitchen where his wife was picking late raspberries under the old window wearing nothing but a bikini top and cut-off shorts. When she heard it was Joe's sister come to visit she came forward smiling, then seemed to remember she was mostly undressed, and passed me the bowl of raspberries while she ducked back into the kitchen to find a shirt.

The smell of raspberries mixed with a kind of salty sandy smell of the walls in the late afternoon sun, and Antonia's wake of sun cream and perfume. I felt the smell of the place, as if it passed into me through my skin rather than my mouth and nose. I felt it like a wave that rose through my feet. I found myself filling up with it, and I knew when it reached my eyes it would drain out in tears. I had to concentrate on keeping it somewhere in my chest as I followed Ted to the back of the house, balancing the raspberries in their bowl, and the smell of them under my ribs.

As we came out into the orchard Ted told me he and Antonia had bought the house from the people we sold it to, who had stayed about ten years. They were both lawyers, and now their daughters were both at law school too, which I guess explained how they had enough money to make it all so beautiful. He said his girls had grown up there, playing in the garden. This was the tree house he had built for them. This was where they kept a donkey called Clive of India, he couldn't remember why. 'Did you ever have a donkey here? No? Maybe it was the people after you. There was a little donkey cart we found in the barn. That gave us the idea. But really, donkeys! They make a lot of noise, and Clive was so bad-tempered we never got him near the cart.' I said no, we'd kept chickens, and ducks. He looked disappointed.

'The donkey cart wasn't from your time? Or before you

maybe? We thought it must be, somehow. No?' As if to jog my memory about the donkey cart, he showed me the restored barn, which was a thing of loveliness, and not in the slightest bit dangerous. All the inventions had been cleared out, and the floor painted. That was how they both knew Joe, who had asked to come and study the inventions in the barn, and helped to catalogue them before they were removed to an obscure museum of technology.

Ted jokingly said that now they had lived there fifteen years he thought some of the village had started to accept them. Fifteen years! That meant he and his wife had now lived there two years longer than I ever did. About as long as my parents ever had. How had that happened? Didn't any of these people realise it was my house?

Antonia came round the side of the building newly dressed in a flowery shirt that tied above the waist and pink linen trousers.

'Come into the conservatory,' she said. 'Let's show you the conservatory we built on the other side! Stay for a cold drink at least, on a day like today!' If the word conservatory makes you think of a white plastic box on the back of a house where the dog's bed and boxes of toys go a bit mouldy, then think again. This was more like an orangery. A botanical garden. An ornate wooden structure with an elaborate pointed roofline and a dragon weathervane. 'Do you remember the weathervane?' said Ted. 'We found it in the barn. I assumed it came from your time here. Or earlier.' I had no memory of a weathervane of any kind. I could see I was a disappointment to them.

Antonia looked closely into my face, trying to trace a likeness to Joe.

'He tamed our rescue dog last time he was here. We couldn't do a thing with him, could we? But he followed Joe around like a shadow. He'd have gone home with him, wouldn't he?' My dog was behaving really badly at this point, trying to eat the horse manure they had put under the standard rose trees. But even without the dog, I think they had me pinned as the prodigal.

Ted turned a series of wooden wheels on the sides of the conservatory to open the wooden windows in the roof, and I dragged my shit-eating dog inside where there was a tray of iced lemon drink with sprigs of my mother's mint balanced on the ice cubes.

Antonia said, we had such fun last time Joe was here, looking for the box of treasure he buried in the garden for the next people to find. He left it under an apple tree, but now it's all gone, long gone, rotten through and through, and we've never found it. The people before us never mentioned it, but they weren't that chatty, were they?

I said, don't look too hard where that apple tree used to be against the hedge, because that's where we buried six chickens one time, some of them with no heads, and that is not the sort of treasure you want to find.

They asked after Edward too, and said they had seen him on that television programme, the one about the medieval village recreation, how the whole village had watched it specially, their very own expert. I said yes, wasn't it good, when in fact I had only seen the second part of it, and he wasn't even in that episode. They said I must be so proud of him, of everything he'd done. I said yes, not many men were single parents in his day, it must have been lonely. They looked confused, so I guess they meant I should be proud of him for the scholarly books and television appearances.

Ted said perhaps I could solve the mystery, why the lawn just beyond the terrace had an outline that rose up in dry weather, the shape of some small building. So we all filed out of the conservatory and followed him around the side of the kitchen wall. And there it was. The palimpsest of our old washhouses, the place we used to pile up my outgrown tricycle and doll's pram and piles of plant pots that would come in handy next year. Nothing but a slightly paler rectangle in the neatly mown stripes of grass.

I got quite excited about these outlines in the grass. I said yes, this was the outside loo. And the pigsty. And then there was a sort of wall here, and I used to light fires inside here for fun. But privies and pig houses are not very romantic. Ted and Antonia looked less enchanted by the minute.

'There were some stories. You know, old stories, about the house. Things your brother would have been too young to remember.' Antonia was looking very hard at the yellowish marks in the grass, and Ted was looking uneasily over his spectacles. Was she trying to ask about ghost stories? Or something about my mother? I wasn't sure.

Besides, now I remembered Susannah, waiting for me at the fairground, so I said, thank you for the cold drink, it's lovely to see the place so beautifully looked after, and dragged my dog away from where he was trying to dig a hole in their immaculate lawn.

I couldn't remember what had been down that side of the house before their orangery. Perhaps nothing. Was that where the fence ran along the edge of the sheep field? Or the broken flagstones of an old terrace pushed apart by the vines that grew up through them? But wasn't that on the other wall? Surely I would have walked past them if I arrived from the river path? But then, their gate was in the wrong place.

Maybe I had walked around the wrong side of the house, and didn't realise. How had it all got so tumbled together in my head? Were my memories all back to front and inside out? I ran back along the path, the flowers for the Green Chapel still in my hand, frightened now that I had misremembered my way; perhaps I was heading away from the church and the fairground like you do in nightmares, the ones where you get further and further away from where you need to be.

I wondered if the ghosts at the Green Chapel would be angry with me for taking their flowers away. I thought of burial rituals then, the ones where the corpse is buried facing the wrong way, so when the spirit climbs out to go back to its old house, it will be facing in the wrong direction and get lost. And of the ritual where the body is buried facing the right way because everyone knows that ghosts turn 180 degrees when they climb out of the ground. And I wondered which kind of revenant I was, the one who was pointed in the right direction or the one who was facing the wrong way, and how, whichever one I was, I had ended up wrong, lost, unable to find my way home.

When had Joe and Edward made a treasure box and hidden it in the orchard for the next owners to find? Why hadn't they asked me to put things in too? Or maybe they had, and I refused. When did they go out into the garden and bury treasure without me? And why had Joe kept his visits here a secret? When had he been staying here, cataloguing the inventions in the barn, charming the lawyers and their rescue dog? Why was I not invited? And why, after all these years, was I still behaving like the naughty child, stomping along the footpath with my delinquent shit-eating dog, fighting back the panic and the tears and the pollen from the cow parsley, wishing I had said something different, something better, or at any rate less bad?

There was a jogger coming up behind me on the path, so I pulled the dog right up into the hedge with me to let her past. A jogger in pink linen trousers and a flowery shirt. Antonia. She stopped to catch her breath, holding out a small envelope.

'Did I drop something? Sorry.' I immediately started checking my pockets for car key, house key, stuff I might have dropped.

'Treasure. After you'd gone we remembered. We did find treasure, thought it must be from the box your brother left behind. There was a magpie's nest. Lots of little bits of tin foil, and this. Ted just thought of it.' She held out the envelope. There was something hard and metallic in one corner of it. Joe had said he left a matchbox car, some Meccano. I opened it. There was what looked like a silver-coloured box, no more than a centimetre square, with leaf-shaped pieces along one side, tarnished with soil and sand.

'Do you recognise it?'

'Sorry, no. I expect Joe will though.'

'Give him our love. Tell him Ralf says hi.'

'Ralf?'

'The puppy.'

'Oh right. Thank you. For the treasure. And the drink.' She turned and jogged back along the path, waving.

I thought about the treasures I had left in that garden, things I could have asked them about, but didn't. I bet those little pieces of tin foil they threw away out of the magpie's nest were the coins I cut out for my Raggle Taggle Gypsies game, things I could throw out of my bedroom window and sing, 'What care I for my money-oh!' Not a box marked treasure under a tree, but a trail of lost shoes and strings of plaited embroidery silks and pipe-cleaner people with stitched-on faces and secret doors to fairy houses carved into the bases of trees and painted with enamel paint in tiny dots on the end of a cocktail stick.

I could have traced the whole plot of 'The Raggle Taggle Gypsies' from my bedroom window where I sang the first verse, looking out to hear the gypsies singing at the gate, to where I kicked off my high-heeled shoes – a-made of Spanish leather-oh – round about the back door somewhere, to where I ran through the grass to ride on the getaway pony, a halffallen-down apple tree strung with baler twine for reins, away to the far field where I could lie under the stars and listen to their beautiful music.

And behind me somewhere, playing the boring role of the left-behind husband, there would be my mother, pretending not to see me, singing in her croaky voice, 'Oh he rode east, and he rode west, he rode north and south also,' galloping into the four corners of the walled garden in her wellies, until she found me and put on her special deep grumpy voice to sing the part of the husband:

How can you leave your house and lands?
How can you leave your money-oh!?

How can you leave your new-wedded
Lord To run with the raggle taggle gypsies-oh?

And I would jump up dramatically out of the grass and put my hands on my hips to sing my reply:

Oh what care I for my house and lands?
What care I for my money-oh?
What care I for my new wedded Lord?
I'll run with the raggle taggle gypsies-oh!

It didn't occur to me for years that my mother's favourite song is all about running away from home, taking nothing with you, not even the shoes on your feet. And even when your husband tracks you down by riding north and south and east and west, you defy him. What do you care for all that stuff? Sheets and feather beds and money and shoes and gold? You would rather lie in the field and hear beautiful singing.

If I could, I would unearth the whole song in props and costumes, from under the stones of their perfect terrace, and in among the roots of the runaway herb beds, and buried deep in the skeletons of six bantams, until I came to the wide open field where I confront my mother, who else, with her desertion. How can you leave your house and land? And your daughter? And your baby?

And as I ran back to the fairground, my throat full of cow parsley and my nostrils full of diesel and hot dog and popcorn, I thought of Susannah riding the Flying Saucers with her new friends, the third one in the little car, the one who is from somewhere else, making up the numbers. I wondered if she was afraid and too shy to show it. I wondered if the others had been kind to her, if they'd said something nice about her hair or her clothes, the way girls do if they want to make friends. What clothes had I got for her that day? Were they the right kind? Had I done her hair the way she liked?

I imagined her high up above the churchyard, her size threeand-a-half feet in second-hand trainers made new with nice laces, looking out along the footpath, watching me run back. Would she want me to stay away a little longer? Or was I already late? And by the time I got back close enough to hear her delighted squeals as she flew round and round above my head, I was mad as hell with my mother.

Go ahead and leave your house and land, your marriage, your money, your uncomfortable shoes and everything they represent, but when you get to the turn in the path and imagine your baby waking without you, and the milk comes whether you like it or not, pulsing out into your clothes, sticking your dress to your stomach, that's when you turn for home. Surely.

But it was never really my mother's favourite song. It was mine. I loved the dressing up, the golden jewels made out of kitchen foil, the high-heeled shoes, the long dress, the baler twine horse, the singing questions and answers to and fro, the game of hide-and-seek in the garden. I guess my mother was sick of re-enacting it, always getting the dull part of the rejected husband, having to stop pegging out washing or kneading bread or pricking out tomato seedlings, and saddle up her imaginary horse to go and be rejected in the orchard.

Now I've had a five-, six-, seven-year-old daughter of my own who loves to play 'let's pretend' I know how often you have to stop what you are doing and slip into the role of a princess or more often a villain, and stomp about the living room roaring and grumping, trying not to lose patience with the whole thing while the rice pan boils over.

I was the one who kept singing about running away with the gypsies. My mother preferred the other story where you have to travel north, then south, then east, then west, where at the end you find what you are looking for, and it isn't your runaway bride, but somewhere to call home.

The girl in that story is bound to the earth by a pair of iron shoes. Much like my own mother in her mud-heavy wellies going out in the pouring rain before the sun goes down to find her last chicken and lock her in safely for the night. It goes like this.

There was once a princess who grew up locked in a tall tower. Or, at least everyone told her she was a princess when they sent up her food in a little basket. But she might not have been. Maybe it was a story she told herself while she was there on her own. No one knows for sure. It doesn't even matter. She longed to see the world outside, but there was no way out.

One day a terrible war came to that country, and the people who used to send her food were all killed or ran away, and besides, there was no food to send up. All the fields were burned and the animals left to starve if they could not get away.

So the girl realised she would have to find her own way out. She could not reach the ground, she didn't have anything she could use for a rope, so she started to dig through the floor. She didn't know how long it might take her, so she had to be careful to make the food she had left last as long as possible.

The further she dug the harder it got, and very soon all her clothes were rags, her hands were torn and rough, and her beautiful hair was so full of dust and clay that it was easier to cut it off. She ran out of food, but she knew her only hope was to go on digging, so she drank the rainwater she collected from the roof, and ate moss and the insects that crawled into the walls.

When she finally dug her way to the bottom of the tower and climbed out of the ground, she didn't look like a princess any more. She met an old woman, as ragged and dirty as herself, and the old woman shared her bread and her campfire with the young girl and gave her this advice: 'You will wear out a pair of iron shoes before you find what you are looking for.'

In the morning the old woman was gone, and on her feet the girl found a pair of iron shoes. They were not comfortable, and she had never had to walk anywhere before in her life, but she found they were stuck on her feet, so she set out on her quest.

She travelled north, then south, then east, then west, working in the fields or anywhere she could earn enough money for food, sleeping in barns and under hedges or sheltering with the animals for warmth, until one day she woke up to find her feet on the ground. Her iron shoes had worn all the way through, and her bare feet were touching the mud.

She was delighted to be rid of the shoes. She looked about her and saw the ruin of an old tower and children were playing around it and climbing over the broken-down walls. The fields around it were planted, and there were farms with chickens and pigs and goats wandering in and out of the yards and rooting about in the hedges.

She asked the children what country it was, and was astonished to hear her own language in their voices. She had heard so many different kinds of voices in all her travels. The children told her the story of a poor girl locked in a tower, and how sad it must be to be locked away like that. They said no one knew what had happened to her in the war.

So she told them how she had escaped, and they were impressed by her, and took her to meet the new king. The new king was pleased to hear she had survived and he welcomed her back to her own country where she lived happily for the rest of her life. And the children kept playing in the ruins of the tower, and telling the story, and no one locked their children up in towers any more.

Okay, so she might have changed the story here and there. Specifically the ending. And possibly quite a bit of the start and middle too. But I found the ending very satisfying. Especially when my mother told me the story, and she looked around her at the end, at her chickens under the trees and the fruit bushes bursting with currants, and she took off her wellies and curled her feet in the grass, and I knew she meant the princess was her, and she had come home, where she could be happy for the rest of her days, and never mind the ruin of a silly old tower that no one remembered any more.

20

The Green Chapel

Solomon Grundy,
Born on Monday
Christened on Tuesday
Married on Wednesday
Sick on Thursday
Worse on Friday
Died on Saturday
Buried on Sunday.
That was the end
Of Solomon Grundy.

Sometimes I forget all about my mother. Whole days go by and I think about other things, things that leave no space for her absence. I do it on purpose: I fix my mind on other things. When I am drawing or painting I forget all about her. I forget about everything. I have to set alarms on my phone to tell me to stop and go to collect Susannah or put the dinner in the oven. And when the timer goes off, and I return to the world around me, there she is again, somewhere out in the margins, a shadowy emptiness, guilt, a door closing just out of sight, the breath of it, something like the smell of the garden, an empty, straw-like taste. Nothingness.

I have gone weeks at a time without talking to her. I have travelled to new places and not thought about telling her what I see there. I have left my unfinished, impossible book about her in the attics of rented houses and failed to climb inside the hatch and collect it at the end of the tenancy. I have graduated without her, found myself pregnant without her to call, taken the first photographs of my daughter and not sent her a copy. I have moved away from the place where I knew her, in every sense. I have put distance between us. Time has put distance between us. All I did was stick around long enough for it to happen.

Forgetting is not the worst thing. Remembering is not the worst thing either. The worst thing is when you have forgotten, and then you remember. It catches you out. You forgot for a moment, a day, a week, a month, but the effect is the same each time you remember. You feel it rushing back around your lymphatic system, and you remember the hurt. And there is a part of you that thinks, perhaps the pain is optional now? What might it be like to live without it? This is treachery. You hate yourself for it.

You'd think I would be used to it by now, the turning up of memories like digging the same ground over and over, picking out shards of the same broken crockery, looking for clues in everything. But for some reason I didn't connect the little silver-coloured box with my mother. It looked too much like a toy. I had no memory of her wearing it. And besides, it was Joe who had hidden a treasure box in the garden.

Susannah and I called in on Edward and Joe on the way back from the Wakes, planning on getting Chinese takeaway with them before we headed home. We were sitting round the kitchen table reading the menu and changing our minds three times when Susannah remembered the envelope.

'Hey, the people at the Old House found some of your treasure.'

'Oh, right. Is it a toy?'

'No, it's a little box. I'll get it from the car.'

Susannah shook it out of the envelope, and a little pile of sand-coloured dust sprinkled over the wrinkled apples in the fruit bowl. Joe picked it up, and turned it over. He slid a clip up one side of it, opened the box, blew out the soil.

Edward said, 'Just a minute. Let me see that.' And right away the texture of the air changed around us. Solidified. Tasted wrong. I watched Edward close his hand over the box and open it again. I was suddenly aware of the age of his fingers, the papery yellow skin, fine white hairs across his knuckles, the very lines of his palm. I put my hand over his, and Joe said, 'What is it?' Edward closed his hand over it again, held one fist in the other, as if he might lose it.

'It was your mother's. She was fond of it. Did they say where they found it?'

'In a magpie's nest, they said. Was she wearing it when she left?'

'No. She'd lost it months before. Before Joe was born, anyway. We looked where she'd been digging but never found it. But then, it's a big garden.'

'I don't remember her wearing it.'

'No? She didn't always.'

Joe held out his hand for it, blew the grains of dirt out of it, slid the tiny catch up and down.

'So the question is, what went inside it? What's missing?'

'It's an amulet. You keep a prayer in it, traditionally. But the paper inside was always getting wet or dirty or something, so she had to keep renewing it. All she put on it was the date, February 10th. She didn't even put his name.'

'That's Jonathan's birthday? February 10th?'

'Yes.'

'Why did she need it round her neck? It's not like she'd forget it.'

'No. She thought it was like a bad spell, having his name on the paper. You know, like naming an effigy. There's supposed to be magic in naming someone.'

'Like in *Rumpelstiltskin*.'

'Exactly.'

'So the date was instead of his name?'

'Something like that. A spell, but not a dangerous one.'

Joe and Susannah exchanged looks. Joe said, 'Looks like we all need dinner. Why don't me and Suzy go and get the Chinese from the end of the road?' I put my hand over Edward's and held on as if we were invalids together, carefully, like very old people, as if we might break each other's skin. After they had left, then come back right away when they remembered the takeaway only accepts cash, and ransacked everyone's wallets and set off again, Edward said, 'She didn't need to wear it to remember him. To remember his birthday.'

'I know,' I said, 'but I think she missed it. She remembered too late. That year, when Joe was a baby, I think she forgot.'

'But she went to the river.'

'Too late. She went on the 23rd. She was thirteen days late.'

I wanted to tell him, no, we always went. We took flowers and a candle in a jar. We sang his special song. She had told me the story of Sir Gawain and his journey to the Green Chapel. I knew it had to be done on the right day. Even if it was raining hard, there was no delaying it. Even if the path was half-washed away.

We often needed an umbrella, so we carried our jam jars and candles and matches and flowers in an old ice-cream box inside the rucksack. We had to wear boots, and even then our feet would be dragged down in the mud. We had to pass through the bottom field where the huge pollarded willows loom like giant cages out of the marsh, the field they call Draconie, the dragon's eye. Past the first bridge, onto the second.

I remember taking a wooden rabbit one time. I don't know why. Perhaps it was my idea. Or perhaps my mother took birthday presents for him. We sang songs. Question and answer songs, though we had to go in single file along the footpath, and if it rained we couldn't really hear the other person through the hoods of our cagoules.

'I'll give you two-oh! Green grow the rushes-oh!'
'What is your two-oh?'
'Two, two, the lily-white boys, clothed all in green ho-ho!
One is one and all alone and ever more shall be, so!'

I never doubted our Green Chapel was the right one, the one Sir Gawain had to find by travelling north and south and east and west like the girl in the iron shoes. It was green, with moss and nettle banks and lichen. It was secret, down a broken path half-fallen into the river. It was a chapel, with names of the dead carved into tablets in its walls. Gawain had to fight wild men and bears and wolves. All we had to fight were strands of bramble and mud and holes in the path left by badgers.

We had to find a sheltered corner to light the candle in the jam jar and lay the flowers on the ground. The bunch of flowers would be plaited together with coloured thread. My mother's voice was croaky, scratchy with a late winter cold. The rain ran down the backs of our coats and under our collars. The candle would go out and have to be relit. The rain poured down my mother's face.

I cannot separate out the visits in my mind, one year from another. It might not always have rained. I might sometimes have held her hand on the path, if it was not too washed away to walk side by side. But now I looked over the memories of that pilgrimage, and I couldn't find one where we had Joe with us.

If we took Joe along, the only year he was alive to go with us, he would have been a tiny baby, and there is no way a pushchair could have got along that path. He would have had to go in his sling, and I would have had the important job of carrying the ice-cream tub of important things.

Joe hated his sling. He always screamed in it. He would have shouted all the way along the river. Maybe we waited until he was asleep, or we left him at home with Mrs Wynne. Or maybe I don't remember taking Joe along the river to the chapel because he never went. Maybe we missed the date. Maybe that was the year we forgot.

With no school timetable, we often lost track of the days at home. Weekends were different because Edward was home. But in between we didn't know one day from another. The radio was always on in the morning, but we didn't listen to it much in the day. There was no calendar of after-school clubs and play dates. And that year my mother had a new baby to look after. She was exhausted, distracted, living from day to day. It's understandable. No one would blame her for missing a date.

I don't know if my brother's ghost was troublesome. Did my mother believe that ghost children grow older? That they grow jealous of their siblings' toys and pets, that they stay at home living alongside the rest of the family, watching all the others get birthday presents and cuddles? That they help themselves to treats from time to time just to let us know they are still there?

The police questions turned out to be the only ones we needed all along. What day and date was it? What path did she take? What was the weather like? What did she carry with her? It was staring us in the face.

And I realised I had been looking in the wrong poem for the answer to my mother's disappearance. All those years reading *Pearl*, going round and round the cycle of consolation, I had not felt very consoled.

I measured out years of grief rereading the story of the stricken man in his garden, arguing with God. I measured the stanzas through my fingers like a rosary, recited their odd sounds in my head, painted endless unfinished series of images of the garden and the bed of herbs, the riverbank of shining mud, the pebbles in the stream bed lit like jewels, the banks crowded with young children in their purgatory white gowns. I followed the dreamer out of the garden down the bottom gate along the river, and woke back in the garden to start my journey over again. And I never felt consoled. All the time I was rereading *Pearl*, I should have been thinking of Sir Gawain and his trip to the Green Chapel.

My mother was exhausted from her new baby, and all the days and nights which rained inside the house and ran into one another like the fields across the flood plain joining one by one to the river until even the hedges were smudges of shadow under the grey water. She was so tired Edward arranged for Mrs Wynne to come out every afternoon to let her sleep for an hour with the baby while Mrs Wynne kept an eye on me and did some laundry or other quiet household tasks that would not disturb them upstairs. She was so tired she did not know what day it was, let alone what date. She was vaguely aware it was February, and the weather forecast still terrible.

What if one day she saw what date it was and found out she had missed his birthday? Would she set out, too late, with no wellies on her feet and no coat against the rain, no candle, no song, no flowers, her hair plastered to her head, her tears washed away in the rain?

Would she get as far as the flooded path, her feet heavy with the mud, the hedges catching on her clothes, her hands full of thorns when she slips and reaches out to grab something? Then what? Will she go to the Green Chapel to plead with the green-faced faery knight, and beg for mercy? The undead are not known for their mercy. The newborn are not known to make allowances. A price will have to be paid. A forfeit exacted.

By the time she gets to the river she might as well be underwater she is so wet. She has lost all feeling in her feet. Her hands are full of thorns and mud. The footbridge is half-submerged. She is beyond caring, walking instead straight through the floodwater, heading for the chapel on the other side. She throws herself on the mercy of the river. She offers herself up to the water. The river shows no mercy. It never does.

The angel child on the other bank has grown into a ten-year-old boy, dressed in the white clothes of the angels, glowing like the wet stones in the bed of the stream. He is telling her to turn back, go back to the garden, keep safely to your side of the stream. He tries to send her back to the reality of life without him but his voice is washed away by the sound of the river in spate, the distance of the dead.

Her ears are full of the heavy water, her eyes are bloodshot with sleepless tears. There is no unthinkable intention. There is no intention at all. There is simply the horror of forgetting, and then remembering. She does not want to leave any of her children behind. She wants to love them all, but one of them is on the other side of that river, and she cannot reach him.

She was not planning to leave us. She loved us. The impulse that drove her out of the door and along the river was not abandonment. It was love for her lost son. The current that took her under the bridge and out into open water was the flood of memory running like poison through her body, the dreadful cold remembering after you have forgotten.

I got up and made us a pot of tea in my mother's favourite brown teapot, and we drank it out of the souvenir mugs from Scarborough that had been in the cupboard when we moved in. It's not much of a funeral, is it? Two people sharing out a pot of tea at the end of the August bank holiday, the sky stubbornly refusing to go dark, the curtains open. No handful of dust, no poetry, no singing. No eulogy, no promise of life everlasting. And it only lasted as long as it takes to fetch a takeaway from the end of the road.

Joe and Susannah blew into the room in a burst of energy and the sweet smell of monosodium glutamate. They set out the foil trays across the table, and Joe picked up my mother's little silver box and said, 'Where shall we keep this, for safety?' and neither Edward nor I could say anything in reply. 'Look, I'll put it in the envelope for now, okay?'

And after we had eaten, Joe said, 'You know how you always say we'll have a funeral if we find something to bury? Well, will this do? Can we bury this? It's about time she had her own stone anyway.'

We can replace the missing paper from inside the silver amulet, his name written down with a gold pen and ink, just like in his special song. We can bury it next to her son's stone, and add one for her. Susannah can choose one of the carved angels from the stairwell and lay it down next to her. I'll sing 'Green Gravel'. We might plant lemon mint, or lavender. Next year at the Wakes her name will be on the list they read out of everyone whose remains have been buried in the churchyard in the past twelve months. Margaret Brown, late of this parish.

21

The Problem with Happiness

Green gravel, green gravel,
Your grass is so green,
The fairest young maiden
That ever was seen.

I'll wash you in new milk
And wrap you in silk,
And write down your name
With a gold pen and ink.

Everyone always wants to know what was making her so unhappy. Why was she so unhappy? They turned the house inside out tracking down her sadness. But they were looking for the wrong thing. In their search for her misery they destroyed the evidence of its opposite. She was happy. I remember her singing. I remember her getting the Moses basket ready for Joe.

I remember her face when she lifted him out of his basket to kiss his nose and make him laugh.

She was happy. That was the trouble. She was so happy that she forgot to be sad. She let her days run into each other, falling asleep on my bed reading *Alice*, forgetting what we read the night before and reading it again, and neither of us caring if she did, forgetting what we had for tea yesterday and making the exact same, laughing at herself for it, falling asleep, feeding the baby, kneading the bread, starting again.

She lost track of the days and she lost track of her sadness. So when it came back at her, it caught her off-guard. It reared up viciously and tore into her with its accusation: how could you forget me? How dare you be happy? And she was too tired and too unguarded and joyful to have any defence against it. It tore her from her happiness and sent her to the river and held her face under the water.

The lane that leads to our old house is called Finsdale. Fin is an old name for the devil. It means the devil's valley. If you ask why, all anyone will tell you is that the river is prone to floods. It was always a dangerous place to cross, in the days before there was a bridge. It does not look like the haunt of the devil. It smells of wild garlic. It is full of nettles. It is dark and tangled and the stink of the garlic stings your eyes when you walk over it and crush the bright leaves under your wellies. The riverbank is sandstone, striped and soft and pinkish, worn away easily into soft curves.

The year she disappeared the stream bed was trodden to red mud with all the boots. The water went thick and red and gritty. The sandbanks on the curve were mashed into deep pitted edges. There was a herd of bullocks in the field by the river. They lined up in a solid bank of warm muscle and breathed their salty hot mashed grass through huge square nostrils at us. They moved like a solid mass of flies, the sound of their hooves thunderous in the quiet.

They tore the riverbank into cloven prints in deep mud, crushing the only evidence they ever found of my mother being there, a single barefoot print on the edge of the river. When the police had finished walking over and over our garden and taking apart the ruins of the barn and emptying the outhouses and searching through the washing baskets and the books and toys and piles of drawings and seed catalogues and interesting things we had dug up in the vegetable plots, it looked as if the bullocks had been through our house and garden as well.

They never found a note. They didn't need to. Everything she left us was a note. The songs she left in my head, the fairy tales, skipping rhymes, conversations with the dead.

The pot of tea in the middle of the table, safely away from her children. The basket of bits of wool she left for me to play with while she went for a nap with the baby. The bread proving in the bottom drawer of the range. The smell of fresh mint through the open window. The washing hanging outside to dry. The bookmark left in *Alice in Wonderland* under my pillow. The pile of colourful pencil shavings in the kitchen bin. The half-knitted striped jumper for when Joe went up a size. The seed catalogues tucked into the corner of the kitchen window.

The note said: I will be there when the baby wakes up. I'll come downstairs to say thank you to Mrs Wynne for peeling the potatoes and ironing the clothes and mopping the kitchen floor. I will be here to bake this bread, and to make a fresh pot of tea. I will carry the washing in from the line and fold it in the basket. I will be here to plant seeds and prick out seedlings and pull up the mint to make space for them. I will finish knitting this jumper and watch my baby grow into it and out of it into the next one.

All the time people trampled the garden and left the washing out to go hard and rained-on and scattered the seed packets and let the bread grow all over the bottom oven and accidentally pulled the knitting off its needle, they undid the note. The note was everything, and everything was destroyed, its meaning lost, the smell of mint gone under the mud, the smell of the bread turned to empty yeast, the catalogues wrinkled up with water, the pages stuck together, *Alice* forgotten, the page unturned, the jumper unravelled.

Everything about my life until the day she disappeared was evidence of happiness. Even our annual pilgrimages to the shrine of my brother – I thought they were a kind of winter picnic. But in the weeks after she left, we turned all of it into its opposite. We turned it inside out to look for the secret unhappiness hidden inside it. By the time we stopped to think, 'Hey, be careful with that, if you take it apart you won't be able to put it back together!' it was too late.

I woke up cold sometime after midnight. There was a draught from an open window on the landing, the low rumble of traffic, something not quite right. The dog got up and walked in a circle in his bed next to me, then lay down again. Susannah? I reached out to put on the bedside light, and changed my mind. The something wrong. Footsteps on the landing, the shuffle of socks on the carpet, soft breath. But Susannah was sleeping over at a friend's house. And the footsteps coming to the bed were not Susannah's. They belonged to my mother. And the faint tang in the air of onion skin and tea leaves and baby powder was the smell of her coming to tuck me into bed at night.

I felt her climb into the bed next to me. I thought, perhaps this means I'm dying. Perhaps that is the meaning of this odd pain in my chest. She has come to get me. I felt relief, that I was off the hook, and it wasn't even my fault. No one could blame me for dying in my sleep.

She smoothed my hair back behind my ears, and I could smell the old kitchen on her hands, the damp stone and sandy garden, the sharp orange tang of coal tar soap, an aftertaste of vanilla, the smell of her own clean skin. I felt her hand on my chest, lightly, as if she could draw out a bruise by levitation. I wanted to say to her, 'I tried, I promise I tried, it's too hard for me, I can't do it any more,' but I had no breath to speak.

Her arms went round me, and my breath came back to me in a sudden wave, all at once, in gulps and starts like an old car starting up from cold. She said to me, 'There's nothing the matter with your heart, Marianne. It's not broken.' And I realised she was right.

Then she was gone, and I rolled easily and painlessly onto the other side of the bed, which was still slightly messy and warm from another person lying there, and the pillow smelled of peppermint and apple peeling and soap, the way it always did when she climbed out of my bed at the end of story time. I moved into the space she had warmed for me, and slept until morning.

Acknowledgements

The trouble with taking my entire adult life to write one small book is that thanks are due to just about everyone I have ever known. People offered me time and space to write in corners of their houses and gardens, among them Jane and Nick Toosey, all the Arvon Centres and Gladstone's Library. Ian Seed at Chester University nursed the book through a PhD programme with remarkable patience. Ellen Edwin-Scott and Sally Toosey read an early draft and helped me to finish it. Peter Buckman at Ampersand Agency agreed to read yet another version of the same story, and Simon Rae never lost faith in the project even when I did. Susie Nicklin and everyone at The Indigo Press believed in the manuscript and turned it into a book. And my children had to live with me while I monopolised the kitchen table and kept at least half my mind in a parallel reality.